Black Spark

Dark Magic Enforcer Book 1

Al K. Line

Get deals and new release notifications first via the Newsletter at www.alkline.co.uk

Chess

I'm to blame, I don't deny it, but how was I supposed to know it would get so out of hand? There was an empty chair calling to me like a cushion amid an ocean of rusty and poisonous nails, so I sat down. I was exhausted, disorientated, probably deranged, and I didn't even remember my own name. Anyway, I won fair and square.

Of course I don't think the poor man deserved to die, and I know it was extreme and very, very stupid, but after the night I'd had it wasn't right to blame me. Not entirely, anyway.

I wasn't myself, at that point in time I wasn't anyone. I was a thing, a dark puppet on corrupted strings, being laughed at and played with, made a mockery of. A vessel sending a message to those from my world—stay away.

It was an accident, I swear. I didn't know what the hell was going on. I didn't even know how I ended up there as it was all a blur.

One minute I was walking, not thinking about anything, the next I came across these people in the park and sat down at a chair. This old guy looked at me, and I knew right away I'd won.

"Do you play?" asked the Grandmaster.

"Now and then," I replied. "At least I think I do."

He gave me a look that annoyed the hell out of me, but I knew I had to stay calm. Something inside told me that, even though my head was as black as his chess pieces, but I knew the game. Chess.

"Your move, white first."

I took my move and, well, I could see the game. I have a touch of the seer, but I usually stay well clear of that as it's a fast route to insanity. Something was off, a lot actually, and I knew the game I was playing like I'd just read it in a book.

Don't ask me how, but it's like the old man knew too, and he took a while to make his first move after mine.

Next came me again. I didn't have to think, I *saw*.

The Grandmaster moved again. He was sweating, acting real nervous, and glanced around repeatedly to see who was watching. Everything had gone silent; the other players and observers knew something was up. One guy was holding his cell phone up, pointing it at us. I moved my piece without thinking, then after what felt like a lifetime he reluctantly made his move.

Snap. I placed my King down.

He looked at me like I was some kind of weirdo, then scowled at the board as if it was life and death, not just chess.

Reluctantly, he picked up his piece, stared at it like maybe there were answers to be found, but there was nothing there but loss. He knew. He did what he could but we both saw the inevitable.

Snap. "Check-mate."

Five moves for me and it was all over.

His teeth clenched, his eyes nearly exploded out of his head, and I could see it coming. But I was tired and confused, half lost to the darkness inside of me. He stood up, eyes unbelieving, shouting, calling me a cheat and a trickster. And then he flipped the board.

I flipped something right back at him.

I punched out, feeling my tight suit jacket chafe as my arm and fist moved on auto-pilot, not trying to hit the guy, but something else.

Then reality spat me back out. I doubled over, sick and feeling like I'd been caught in a stampede of a thousand trolls racing for a pile of free chalk. My vision went, my head kind of contracted, every part of me hurt and my limbs felt like lumps of burning iron. You think a hangover is bad? You've never felt anything like this.

Using strong magic is like drinking so much alcohol that your brain is dessicated, dried up and cracked open like a coconut, the fluid seeping out in sick black blobs full of poisonous venom that jumps back in through your eyes and trickles down your throat to burn your belly like a thousand hot chillies. But worse.

I ran. Staggered would better describe it, I guess.

The Grandmaster was dead. Everyone was going nuts, and I just ran, tried to hide. I was lost, alone, confused, taken by the sickness. And afraid. I had no idea who I was or what I'd done, how I'd done it or why I was so out of it.

Why was I so sick? What had happened? Was any of it real?

My clothes were dirty, my skin crawled like my veins were full of scalding wax, my palms itched so bad I wanted to rub them on razors just to ease the hurt, and I was numb inside, empty of my own self.

Somebody had done this to me.

I just had to find out who, and why.

*

They call me Black Spark, Dark Magic Enforcer, even though my name is Faz Pound, a.k.a. Spark to most that know me, or know of me. And if you meet me I'll shake your hand, smile nicely, and be on my way, but chances are you will never have that dubious honor.

I don't exactly allow Regulars to see me at all. I'm the everyman, the person you can never recall, the man you can neither describe nor remember. I walk the line between worlds and I live in both, but am only truly memorable in one, and it isn't yours.

I'm a shadow, a blur of a person. A dark mist in your consciousness and that's the way I like it.

Magic isn't all shiny lights and big pots of gold, it's dark and dangerous and you don't get a warm fuzzy glow when you use it.

You feel sick to your stomach, as though every demon in the netherworlds is trying to claw its way up into the world via your guts.

It burns, it hurts, it makes you want to puke, and there is no nice blue glow of magic that tickles your fingertips and dances in the air like fae off on vacation, sprinkling priceless dust as they go.

What you get when you use magic, when you draw it from the Empty, is a sinkhole of horror as insanity tries to take you, and if you're caught in the crossfire you'll probably want to rip out your insides and claw at your face and poke your eyes out with sticks. Blunt ones.

That's just if you happen to be close. If it's directed at you, well, you are seriously out of luck, my friend. I can use it, not that I particularly like to, but it's there, part of who I am. I'm adept, and it comes with the job. I'm good at my job. Usually.

Sorry for being so dramatic, but that's what stories are for, right? Going on a journey, learning new things, having fun at someone else's expense—in this case mine—and hopefully rooting for the good guy. Yeah, that's me, honest it is. Sure, I have my faults, but I am the good guy.

Nobody messes with me and gets away with it, though. Nobody.

So, here's what I found out once the sickness passed and I could think straight.

The World's a Lie

The world, this place we get to sink or swim in for a blink of a god's eye, is not what most people imagine. You think of it as making sense, of everything having a reason, and obeying these laws you've been taught in school or by your parents—all that stuff. I hate to be the one to tell you, but it's all nonsense.

Not quite a lie, but not the whole truth either.

It's worse than you can possibly imagine. A lot worse. There are demons, there are vampires, there are beautiful and terrifying fae with their ears that make me go weak at the knees. Trolls, goblins, gremlins—endless true Hidden—and all manner of humans with access to the Empty in varying degrees.

There are even unfortunate, but friendly in their own way, zombies, although call them that and some will eat your brains and insist they aren't actually dead. Who knows, maybe they aren't. I've never really wanted to find out.

Oh, there are wizards too, and that's me, a goddamn wizard! No, I don't have a pointy hat, and there's no wand or cat or any of that nonsense. And there are no flowing beards—at least not for me anyway—and I sure as hell don't wear robes.

Suits from the nineteen sixties are my preference. Originals that are tight fitting and black. I wear winklepickers, those pointy shoes that look cool as hell, and I always, always, wear a nice clean pair of underwear. I favor white socks and a red shirt, sometimes white if I know I'm not going to get into any bother for a while. So, usually red it is.

Home is the United Kingdom and that's where this story takes place. More specifically, Cardiff.

This magic we use encompasses so many different facets I hardly know where to begin. It's the dark underbelly of reality that remains hidden. Why? Because there are codes, there are rules, the Law, and if you break it, reveal any of our secrets, and I mean any, to Regulars, then you are in serious trouble. Best-case scenario? There isn't one. Worst-case scenario? You wouldn't believe me if I told you. That's why I freaked out after what I did to the Grandmaster.

*

My running was too much, so I slowed to a walk with my guts churning, my head ready to split in two, and a sinking feeling in my belly I'd just done the one thing I wasn't supposed to.

I still knew little more than my name, and that I wasn't feeling quite myself. Beyond that it was mostly a blur. A total blur, actually.

I had no clue what the hell was going on, where to go, or what I was doing.

That, my friend, is not the position you want to be in when you've just blasted someone with the dark arts and know you shouldn't be drawing attention to yourself.

Somehow, I was in a park. One of those nice green spaces that everyone goes to on a summer's day and has picnics, or walks their dog, smooches with their girlfriend or boyfriend and drinks booze, soaking up the rays and feeling great about life.

But this is the UK and it may be summer, but it's a British summer, meaning it was gray, overcast, and drizzling. The kind of rain that soaks you through even though it hardly seems to be raining.

Not me. I was sort of fizzing. I didn't even notice at first, but I was getting weird looks and some little kid pointed at me, then tugged at his mum's skirt and said, "Man all fizzy," and I felt a little self-conscious so looked at my arms. He was right, I was fizzing. And I wasn't wet.

Things were far from right, as under normal circumstances Regulars would never point me out. My life slowly returned to me, but the night before, and that morning, were a blank.

I was supposed to be the everyman, there but not there, a tiny taste of background magic always present.

Enough to make me and those in my world be just about invisible to the nice folks that know nothing of us, our lives, our ways. Not enough to make me sick, just a taster. As much a part of me and my kind as breathing —or not, in some cases. But it wasn't working. People were taking notice, they could see me. I didn't know much, but I knew that was bad.

Running again felt like a good idea, so I ran, like I was afraid of the little dude. Maybe I was, but I was scared of just about everything at that moment, including myself. I'd just killed someone because he was a sore loser, and that wasn't who I was, how I normally acted.

Worse, I knew I'd done something orders of magnitude more damaging than kill a man. I'd unleashed something, and wouldn't just get a wrap on the knuckles for it. A disguise, I needed a disguise, and somewhere to lie low and come to my senses.

My body felt odd, not really mine, and I realize I'm acting anything but cool, and that I'm sticking out like an imp in a bowl of milk. My guess is that the police will be on the scene, and it'll be all over the news. Bits and pieces of my life are coming back, but everything's jumbled. Not just that, it's as messed up as a vampire at a dorm sleepover.

There was a club, there was drinking, but that wouldn't explain why I was out in the early morning stumbling across people playing chess on the edge of the park.

The need to get out of the open overwhelms me. I need the cover of the streets, I need to blend in, and more than anything else I need to remember what the hell led to me doing something so stupid, so cruel. So unforgivable.

As I slow, and act all casual like I'm off to work or taking in the depressing, polluted air that stinks even though I'm surrounded by grass and trees, I take off my suit jacket, fold it carefully, and notice with total surprise that my damn arms are covered in intricate tattoos that stop me in my tracks. I hold out my arms like I'm waiting for someone to throw me a ball.

What the hell is all this?

My arms are pale, slim but well-muscled in that scrawny yet powerful kind of way that a lot of women think is hot—at least I like to think they think that anyway—and the veins are prominent. Blue and popping.

But that's nothing compared to the swirling tattoos that start at the knuckles, wrap around the back of my hands and writhe and dance up my forearms, across my bulging biceps—okay, they are more like two hard-boiled eggs—and disappear under the short sleeves of a very nice red shirt. I think it might be silk. At least I have taste.

As I look at them, they pulse almost imperceptibly, and move, as though they are alive, writhing like they want to get free. And they are black. Or is it blue? I'm still not sure.

It's a weird color, like it's so deep and dark it's the opposite of light, but different. Does that make sense?

Let's say you are in a room and there is no light. None. No windows, no doors, and everything inside it is black. Black walls, black floor and ceiling, and you are black too. Now, add in the darkest blue you can imagine, so dark it's black but not black, well, that's what the ink looked like. But it was one tattoo.

It swirled and danced and wriggled and crawled up my arms, then crept under my shirt like someone had gone wild with a marker pen and had some serious talent to go along with it.

There was no time to check how much of me was covered, as even in my dazed state I knew ripping open my shirt wasn't the best way to lay low.

It was the buzzing, that was it. The buzzing because of what I'd just done. Using whatever it was I used to kill that guy. I'd just murdered someone! I felt bad, sick and like the worst kind of nasty, I honestly did. He was a cranky old sod and acted out of order, but killing a human being, an innocent man, it is beyond criminal. Yet I also felt removed, like I was a different species or something.

My nature was different. I wasn't a human, or not just a human being at any rate.

It's the price we pay, and that feeling never goes away. There's no turning back, though. Once you embrace this Hidden world, it takes a hold of you and it will never let you go.

I started walking again as I heard the sirens of police cars and ambulances.

My breathing was shot to pieces so I focused on that, steadied my heart rate by looking inside and telling it to behave. It worked, so I knew I had some seriously awesome powers. Okay, that was something to go on. As my pulse slowed, so the tattoos fell back into place, becoming interesting markings but not looking like they were getting ready to boogie the night away either.

All hell broke loose as a helicopter flew low overhead, then another, and another, TV station logos emblazoned on the sides.

It was time to get out of the open, figure out what the hell was happening.

I needed a disguise; where were the stores?

A Sacrifice

Turns out the park was pretty small, and only ten minutes from the main shopping center of Cardiff, the capital of Wales. It's a strange country, and a somewhat perplexing and often archaic region where all the signs and literature are written in both English and Welsh, even though it's only mid and north Wales where anyone actually speaks the language, and then few as a first language.

But Cardiff is in south Wales, right by the coast, with regenerated harbors, the mud washed away, and rotten timbers long ago hauled out of sight, replaced with more shiny buildings of steel and glass than can be healthy—that's progress for you.

It's where I live. It's home. Some would say it's even cosmopolitan. There are outdoor cafes and you can walk the streets safely at night as long as you avoid certain areas.

There are parks and green expanses aplenty here. Many on the east side of the city connect to the main

Roath Park via a series of community-orientated spaces with rose gardens, open fields for sports, play areas and more. It all leads to a huge boating lake, with ducks and ice-cream vans—even when it's raining, which it always is—and it's close to the city center too.

Feeling like someone had kicked me in the side of the head while wearing dirty and insanity-stained rugby boots stolen from a three centuries old corpse, I left the scene of my crime behind me, heading down to the smaller parks where there were less people and away from the swarming media and police, where I'd killed somebody for being a bad loser.

I was still fizzing like an out-of-date bottle of Pepsi with a slow leak—it seemed I had a real aversion to getting wet—but it was so subtle nobody would notice unless they were real close. I didn't intend to let that happen again.

Things went from bad to worse.

"Who's been a naughty boy?" came a voice from up above me. What the hell, up above?

"There's going to be trouble," came another annoying sound, this time a man.

Something was off with their vocal cords, like they were talking but breathing out at the same time—it's hard to explain. I didn't even flinch. Yeah, tough guy, right? Not really, I just knew it was what would be called normal in my usual life—if I knew what that was.

"Go away, I'm busy," I said, staring up at the two "people" sat in the tree with their legs dangling over a branch like they'd been there for hours waiting for me.

"Not as busy as you will be. Somebody wants to see you," came the strange lilt of the woman.

She wasn't quite right, the guy either. They were intense somehow, and everything else faded away like an extreme case of tunnel vision, or the way you are just drawn to some people. An inexplicable presence or charisma. But this wasn't in a good way, this was in a run-away-as-these-dudes-are-messed-up way.

"Who?" I couldn't help myself. At least I was getting somewhere. Maybe.

"Who do you think?" said the man, voice almost hypnotic, his words trying to squirm into my head.

I had no idea what he was talking about.

My tattoos danced about my arms as if alive at their presence, and I felt something slam down hard in my head—a rusted steel shutter stopping them getting in and making me do things I didn't want to.

"He's doing it again. So annoying," whined the woman. They clearly didn't appreciate the denial of entry.

"We'll be seeing you soon," said the man.

They jumped down and stood in front of me, scowling at my arms and at me in general, like I was a disappointment.

I guess I was.

I thought it would be a fight there and then. They smiled this weird smile at me, all exposed teeth, sharp and pointy canines just like you'd expect. It was an act —who smiles so their teeth show like that? They looked stupid. They also looked freaking terrifying.

There was an almost overwhelming urge to turn around and see who was staring at me. Like that funny feeling that washes over you sometimes when you are somewhere incongruous, maybe in the newsagents buying a paper and you half expect the bulbous-headed Toad King to peek out from behind a shelf and lick his lips. Or is that just me?

These were not pretty, mesmerizing characters, they were people you knew deep down in your bones were wrong. Their minds were on a different plane to mine and their movements were strange—like a few frames were missed out, making them jerky, running on a different frequency. They looked too old, as if they were weary but had no intention of giving up. Ever.

I brushed past between them, a false bravado. My head was not ruling my decisions. There was this aura about them, like you could lose yourself in their eyes for eternity. They were waiting, waiting to drag me under and take me. No way.

As I moved past, there was one hell of a tingle in parts I really didn't want to get involved, not with me being on the run and all.

"See you soon," said the woman, and they laughed as I picked up speed. I turned a few moments later. They were gone.

That's vampires for you, always got to be dramatic.

Yes, I know. You're thinking, hang on, vampires, in the day, and not bursting into flames? Not gorgeous and impossible to resist? Nope, they were nasty looking, gave me the creeps, and had no problems coping with what passes for daylight and summer around what the locals refer to fondly as "Wet Wales," and for good reason.

So how did they do it, these supposed ghouls of the night?

Magic. From the Empty.

It's not a place, not a thing, it's all there is when you get right down to it. It's the darkness behind matter that makes us all. It's what drives us, what allows us to be alive at all. This is the essence, that mysterious first flip of the switch that turns a collection of cells, or in some cases rocks or the air itself, into something more.

It can be used; brought to life; change you. Like, I'm a wizard, although I don't care for the name. I don't think of myself like that. I'm just a kick-ass part time enforcer for the UK Dark Council, more specifically for Mage Rikka. But he doesn't own me, I'm what they call an Alone.

It's the name they give to those like me, sentient beings that aren't part of a coven, a sect, a family, or whatever any particular species, race, creed or collective calls itself—as if it makes a difference in the long run.

I answer to no man, woman, or entity. Well, that's not strictly true, but I'm not part of any of that nonsense. I will not be classified, categorized, or cauterized—I grew out of gangs a long time ago; it all seems so juvenile.

But it has its drawbacks, this life I lead by choice, like when you kill someone and show the world magic exists and a couple of freakoid vampires come to taunt you and you don't know who you are or what to do next.

Picking up speed once more, I got out of the damn parks, crossed a road without getting hit by a bus, and entered the outskirts of the city.

*

Ten minutes after walking through soaked and depressing streets lined with terraced, red brick Victorian houses—some with flaccid spiders of smoke clawing their way out of black chimneys even though it was summer—and crossing the main road that led to the city center, I was feeling a lot better.

I had my bearings, remembered that I lived in Cardiff and, most importantly at this moment, I knew where the pharmacy was.

Time to get a bit of a disguise going before the hunt was on for me and I got into even more trouble.

The shopping district was packed, so chances were high this was the weekend. Who cared? I had more important things to worry about, at least I assumed I did.

Bing-bong.

I nearly lost it right there, but it was just the damn door making that weird noise to tell the woman behind the counter someone had come in. It was off though, like the batteries needed changing. The noise bounced around my head like a half-deflated beach ball. Stuff like that must drive you nuts. How many times would it happen every day?

The place was busy. That's the damp Cardiff air for you. Everyone always has the sniffles, or a chest infection, and you can't walk five paces without someone coughing something gross into your face. I don't need to worry about that though—perks of being the Black Spark and all.

I got what I wanted from the shelves after wasting precious minutes hunting around—why is there always so much choice in these places?—and stepped up to the counter.

Money! Did I have any? Maybe I was down on my luck, or homeless, or one of those people that never carries it so they can annoy everyone else and amass a fortune by pleading poverty. I patted down my jacket pockets, then quickly put it on as the woman was looking at my arms funny—nice move, Faz.

There was a cell phone, a wallet, and a slip of paper. I tried not to gulp at the contents of the wallet— money somehow permeating my fog of amnesia as I could see I was loaded—and gave a note to the woman.

After giving me my change, she asked if I wanted a bag. I said, yes, and she asked for five pence. She looked at me funny over the top of her glasses. Maybe I pulled a face, or maybe she looks at everyone like that.

I'd forgotten that you had to pay for bags now or carry your purchases loose. Why didn't she ask me before I paid? I changed my mind on principle, declined her offer, and stuffed the items in a pocket.

Back on the street, I picked the closest McDonald's, fought through the carnage of plastic food and plastic containers and plastic smiles of parents with pleading eyes silently imploring, "Save us. Is there nowhere else left to eat now our city is 'cosmopolitan?' Is this all there is?" and hurried through to the back where the toilets hid to deter passersby from braving the morning melee, instead deciding a bursting bladder was a small price to pay for freedom.

And, please don't think bad of me, but I went into the disabled toilets. It was the only one where I could have a room to myself and I could lock it so no one came in. Honest. Look, I may be, well, me, but I'm not that callous.

Jacket off, goodies on the sink, and ignoring the handsome but rather haunted and, I admit, freaked out and no-wonder-the-lady-in-the-pharmacy-looked-at-me-weird face, I took a deep breath and began cutting.

My hair. My beautiful, black, shiny, straight as an imp's ear, gorgeous hair. I cut it all off. Hacked away like a lunatic let loose in a barber's shop with instructions to "have at it." You should have seen it, my hair was the business. Makes me cry just to think about it.

Soon I was down to what I guess you would call urban chic. In other words, it looked like I'd cut my hair myself in a McDonald's toilets with shaky fingers while my eyes refused to focus and felt like I'd washed them in gravel—the bad kind, not the happy gravel we usually all love to use.

To complete the "style," it was also obvious I'd gone all out and cut my locks with a pair of scissors for left-handers. How the hell that happened I will never know. But the cut was all the rage, so why not? Mind you, I didn't know that until later, and all I felt was like I'd committed the second truly terrible act of my so far very not at all fun morning.

Next came the peroxide.

Five minutes later, after sticking my head under the tap and then the drier—that made me feel like I was a dog sticking my head out the window on a car journey and wondering if my tongue was sticking out too—I looked like a new man. Not a better one, just a different one. I also found I had a mole on my neck.

Gone was the dark, mysterious stranger, hello, blondie. It was all right, I guess. In fact I'm getting used to it. Kind of.

Now, about that note.

Putting the Pieces Together

As I walked down the street, feeling strangely exposed without the familiar tickle of hair at my neck, and wondering if the blond clashed with my shirt, I dug out the paper from the inside jacket pocket and unfolded it.

It was a receipt, just not one you are likely to have ever had. This was for services rendered, or maybe not, I couldn't recall. But it explained the cash in my wallet and the memory loss. I'd taken on a job, and clearly it hadn't gone quite as expected.

There are a lot of us, enforcers, cleaning up the mess of others, dealing with people or species that get a little too carried away with what I'm going to stick to calling magic, although it's a word that doesn't do it justice or even hint at the truth. Let's say those with the ability to harness the Empty, that's closer to the reality of it anyway. Those known as Hidden, and for good reason.

I may be an enforcer but I am not a killer. Yes, I've killed, but what happened in the park is not my usual behavior. I'm a bit of a softy really, although if you looked at me you'd see this cool, calm, kick-ass dude who doesn't get bothered by much at all and is always ready for action, but that goes with the job. It's not who I am.

This guy does not go around kicking and punching people, telling them to hand over their cash, or else. I'm an enforcer, tasked with keeping us safe and upholding our, albeit often strange, rules—like the law but without the uniform or the need to fill out forms. A good guy.

Or I was.

Now it had all gone to hell because I'd killed someone, and done the worst thing possible in our Hidden world where bad shit happens all the time but nobody in the Regular world knows anything about it.

I'd let the undead cat out of the coffin, and this was exactly what I was employed to stop happening. It's who I am. It's my identity. It's me.

I've got a special talent. One I wouldn't wish on anybody. I have the ability to suck the Empty right out of you and send it back where it came from. It doesn't work on true Hidden, creatures born wholly of magic, and I can't just stare you down and BAM! you are normal again, but if you are, or were, human, then I can take the magic away and leave you empty inside.

What I do is deal with those that get a little cocky or carried away with their use of magic, risking exposure for themselves and the rest of us.

Except, and this is where things start to make sense, it takes a hell of a lot out of me. So much so that I often lose a few hours afterward, as the only way to get away from the insane pain, the sickness so deep it makes my bones weep, and the feeling of being ripped to bits by a load of annoyed trolls who then hand my still conscious carcass over to a shortage of dwarves, who know for a fact I stole their gold, is to sink down deep into blackness, cry for Grandma, and try to forget I was ever a person.

Which I was. Still am to some extent.

It explained the memory loss that suddenly came back to me when I opened the scrap of paper and realized I'd been on a job. Hopefully it had been successful, but judging by the state of me and what I did I wasn't so sure.

"Hello, Spark."

"Uh-oh."

"That's a new look. Not trying to hide from us are you?" said one of the goons.

Yeah, you guessed it, more vampires. But these weren't like the two relative beauties I met earlier, these were old dudes. Not in appearance, but in actual age. A few hundred years at least, so they were still fine walking around in the daylight, if you could call the weather daylight.

The proper old ones, like thousands of years and more, the bosses, the Heads, they keep well away from the light. They sleep through the day or rest somewhere suitably dark and vampire-like, half-dead until the sun sets and they come to life and are pretty much invincible as people. Not that people is really the best way to describe them.

Younger vampires are okay with being labeled human, or ex-human, but the old ones, the ones that have thrived in the shadows for centuries, even millennia, they will rip out your throat if you refer to them as anything but vampire.

They see themselves like butterflies, emerging from the chrysalis of an almost forgotten human being to become what they are now, and you would no more call a butterfly a caterpillar than you would an old vampire a human being.

Are they dead, these bloodsuckers? No, not really. They use blood magic to remain what they are, and that is pretty much immortal. But such a gift comes at a high cost, more than most are ever willing to pay, and the charge is your humanity.

Yes, I'm not exactly a regular guy, but I know what's right, and wrong—killing the innocent—and I have a lot to answer for because of what I've done, but at least I know the difference. And besides, something happened to make me do what I did. I'm not usually a homicidal chess player, honest.

So, the goons.

"Hi Bret. Hi Bart," I said casually. "Fancy meeting you here. Doing some shopping are you?"

Bret and Bart stared at me, with those spooky as hell eyes serious vampires have, not that many of them are jolly. They aren't big conversationalists, although once, in a rather unexpected outpouring of more than a few syllables each, they'd explained why they had ditched their Chinese names at the turn of the century and insisted on Bret and Bart now—to make themselves more modern.

Nothing crazier than a vampire, apart from a Chinese vampire. Okay, apart from the Welsh, they are proper crazy. Must be the confusion about the signs, or the damp.

"Um, okay. Nice chatting, see ya." I moved to step around them, which was quite a distance, but I knew it was no good, and besides, there's no getting away from these guys once they are given a job.

The twins may look like lumps of Chinese granite, all roughly chiseled features and way too much time spent in the gym to make up for their five foot nothing stature, but they are not to be trifled with. And anyway, I knew who had sent them after me, and to be honest the alternative wouldn't be much better.

Many Hidden would be baying for my blood the moment what I did hit the news or the underground networks, so in a way it was a relief. The kids from earlier were just playing, knew better than to try anything, but the twins, they would fight if they had to. Although I couldn't see that they would have been given orders to mess with me in the middle of the street on a busy Saturday, if it was Saturday—I was in no mood to find out.

Did I go along quietly with the Chinese vampires? Hell no. I knew they wouldn't be at their best in the daylight as they were a few hundred years old. Enough had come back by now for me to know who I was and a little of what I, and they, were capable of. I was an enforcer, but I was also an Alone.

An Alone has drawbacks, the main being you don't have others with you to help focus magic, and numbers are always good. But it has advantages too, like the fact people who can do what I do are pretty damn selfish and not very nice people.

Don't get me wrong, there are a lot of lovely people who can use magic, and some even live relatively normal lives, but most don't. Once you understand our world it's easy to see why.

I steeled myself, not really in the mood for any meetings until I found out why I'd done what I did, and could think of a way to not get killed for it. Maybe by Bret and Bart's boss, or my own, and readied myself for the sickness.

Even thinking about drawing power from the Empty made my guts churn and my palms sweat, but I went with it, let it build, let the darkness envelop me and I felt my tattoos swell with the power.

The nauseating dark magic spread from my knuckles up my arms, across my shoulders and down my torso, just as I felt it come from my feet, writhe along my calves, scamper up my thighs like a hairy-legged giant centipede craving the dark and moist most private parts I owned, and it all met at my navel.

It meant I was covered head to toe in the ink, and I'll have to show you some time. It's pretty impressive and it hurt like hell getting it done, but that was long ago, a memory so distant it may as well be from another life, another person—which isn't far from the truth.

The ink helped me prise open the door to the darkness where the magical forces that permeate the Universe abide, and made more possible than the bag-laden and desperate looking shoppers around me could possibly know.

As the sickness descended, and my heart felt ready to explode, I not so much vanished as faded from memory and sight. If you were witnessing it then I wouldn't be all see-through like a ghost, you'd just not really take any notice as I was there but not there. Like the most nondescript person you could ever imagine. You wouldn't be able to describe me, you wouldn't even remember you'd seen an unmemorable person, I just faded from the world most folks live in.

My head felt like the bone was contracting, as if the twins' muscular fingers were clamped down hard like two Asian vices. My throat was as rough as sandpaper, bile rose, and my body screamed as I faded to nothingness. I stepped to the side and was about to leg it, when Bret, or Bart—I'm never sure which is which—grabbed me by the upper arm and said, "Don't think so, Spark. The boss wants a word. You've been a naughty boy, real bad. Come on."

See, that's the problem with your proper, world wise vampires—it's hard to fool them. They live their lives in the shadows, feed off the magic in everyone, even you, even your dog. Not that they do anything to dogs but keep them as pets mind you. Um, apart from the vampire guard dog ones. Anyway, my disappearing act was a waste of time with them, a waste of time full stop, but you can't blame a wizard for trying.

How was I to know that what I'd just done was my usual state of being when out in normal company? I was still confused and not really myself, and it wouldn't work on vampires anyway. And no, I wasn't about to get all Black Spark on them and shoot the bad stuff out my fingers or anything.

I was in enough trouble already, so killing, if I was lucky, two short Chinese vampires in the high street would get me into more trouble than I was prepared to deal with.

I snapped back to solidity and sighed. "Okay, let's go." I tried not to throw up and swallowed foul tasting liquid as Bret and Bart led the way. I walked in-between them; I wasn't going anywhere without them.

Hey, don't judge me, I'd had a bad day, and like I said, I'm not really a fighter, and certainly not a killer. Just because I do some work for the most powerful wizard in the country doesn't mean I'm invincible. Nobody is. Everyone has their weaknesses, and one of mine is two badass vampires carved from granite, even if they are called Bret and Bart. Yeah, I know, what is with that?

We walked through the city, down the high street, rounded the corner past a tiny church and cemetery right there in the center, went down the alley past Spillers Records, the oldest record store in the world—still there, still selling vinyl—and weaved our way out of the city center.

It's a small place, and soon enough we were getting into a car. Bret and Bart squeezed in either side of me in the back, their heavily muscled thighs making me have to close my legs like I didn't need to do the man thing and open them wide like all blokes do out of principle.

For the entire journey nobody said a word. To amuse ourselves we played the timeless game of who-can-open-their-legs-the-widest, and the driver, a new kid I'd never seen before, took us out of the congestion and up to Taavi's home.

It had been a bad morning, and it wasn't going to get any better. I hadn't even seen my boss yet, so I knew it would be a long day. I also had to figure out what the hell had made me act so out of character.

The one saving grace was that I was finally back to being me. Memories flooded in. I was thinking my usual deep and intellectual thoughts, and sure, there were pieces missing from the night before and the early morning, but I knew who I was, felt like I was whole again.

I was back!

I was also a disgrace to my kind. It kind of put a downer on the whole self-realization—it made it hit home all the harder just what it was I'd done.

I was an enforcer, supposedly one of the best, and it was my job to see to it, no matter what, that magic remained underground and nobody ever heard about it. Yet there I was, the one that had finally exposed it to the world—that's the problem with the modern age, everyone has a damn phone and bloody camera.

There's no privacy. It sucks.

An Admission

Why do we need enforcers? Because the Hidden are a rather impulsive and often dangerous lot, that's why. Magic does funny things to you, and as there is no end of magic, and ways it can be used, there is also no end of danger and trouble to clear up.

It's the usual thing really. Nobody "normal" is supposed to know about all this, because if they did all hell would break loose and the world would end up blowing itself to bits.

Can you imagine if your neighbor, your boss, the postman, or everyone, could search deep down inside themselves and call on powers that would turn your mind to mush or your intestines to goo? Right. Stuff would get messy really fast.

So there's a pact, an agreement. What happens in our world, stays in our world. No leaks. None. It remains Hidden and for good reason. There are good guys and bad guys, but mostly it's all gray. Just like regular folks, everyone has a good side and a bad side.

It just gets a lot more serious for us, what with the ease with which we can all kill each other. But that's the life we live, and we keep to the rules, the Law. Mostly.

If you saw me I'd be what some would call a bit of a throwback. I like retro suits and red shirts, and I had nice, long black hair, although as you already know I'm going through a blond phase at the moment.

The money I earn is okay, nothing to write home about, but I don't have what you would call a "normal" job. I set my own timetable, usually, and don't have a boss in the strictest sense of the word, although we all answer to somebody.

I can freelance, and have, but Rikka is who pays me most often, and that's no surprise as he's the numero uno, the big kahuna, the big cheese, otherwise known as one mean dude who rules the roost. In this case meaning he is in charge of ensuring that us wizards, or other users of the Empty, tow the line and keep our business away from normal folk.

I help him with that, and others, by taking away the magic the miscreants have, or are using. All the time they put into gathering and perfecting such power will have been for nothing.

I do it to keep the peace, maintain order, and to get paid, and it usually works out fine. Imagine me as the guy that comes to take away the man hiding in your cupboard ready to scare the wits out of you and steal your soul. Something like that anyway. I deal with those that go off the rails and can't keep the magic inside any longer, and I send them back to the Regular world without a hope of ever returning to ours.

I keep it all under wraps, rein in those that get out of control, and I do not kill Grandmaster chess supremos.

Apart from one.

Okay, there have been a few other "incidents," but I've never done it to anyone that wasn't seriously bad news, which is why I'm in trouble right now. You absolutely do not, under any circumstances, ever go around killing Grandmasters in the park on Saturday and get your dark arts plastered all over the news.

About this magic, I hear you ask, sounds nasty. Well, yeah, it is. For humans. It's not ours. We steal it, as we can't help ourselves. It belongs to the true Hidden. There are no happy-clappy, nice white witches and wizards that thrive only on pure, clean energy, there is just the Empty, the forces that make up the entire nature of the Universe, and it's all pretty cold, and it's all the same. It's just this essence, this energy that our kind can harness. At a price.

If you looked at me, and I let you "see" me, then you'd think I was late twenties, maybe early thirties, well turned out if a little out there with my choice of clothes, but that's not really the case. Those of us involved in the Empty don't live regular lives no matter how hard we may try, and our lifespan is different to other's.

I was born in 1901, right at the turn of the twentieth century, and trust me, things are much better now than they were then, even if the place is a little crowded and smelly compared to so long ago.

Magic may hurt like hell, but it has its benefits, and one of those is that it can seriously dent the aging process. Not immortality like the vampires—although I don't like that term, as they aren't freaked by crosses and don't need an invite before they suck the blood out of your eyeballs—but you can live a long time if you let magic into your life.

Let's just say I've seen a lot, ended up crossing the line from Regular to wizard some time ago, although it was always inevitable, and my favorite era is the nineteen sixties.

Now, where were we? Ah, Chinese vampire goons.

Big Vampire Boss

You know that vision you have of a head vampire? All pointy teeth, pale skin, bloodshot eyes, probably handsome as hell and tall with flowing hair? Well, it isn't like that. Not for the head honcho, not for most vampires.

You see, to be in charge, and more importantly, to stay in charge, takes a vampire of incredible power and unimaginable age. Taavi is all of that, and then some. The old bit, not the handsome and all mesmerizing bit, although he is mesmerizing, in a scary-enough-to-make-Regulars-go-instantly-insane way.

You don't get to live for over two thousand years sucking blood from human beings and not become something unlike anything else on the planet. There aren't many this age, a few on each continent if that, but the old guys rule, and they will find your weak spot, slither into your mind as easily as a wayward thought, and you are theirs.

They are masters of their art. One lapse of focus in their company and you will find yourself staring into yellow eyes with the sorrow of the entire history of the world there for you to see, unforgiving and uncaring as they take what's yours so they can live another day, month, or year, depending on their age.

Taavi is ancient, and I don't want to think about how often he needs to feed, or the number of lives he has taken. After all, these old ones have had a lot of time to get the infrastructure in place and gather a lot of loyal followers, although, being vampires, you can't really trust them.

Those that manage to survive in the backstabbing, vindictive, violent and distrustful world of their kind thrive like you would not believe. Once strong enough to kill others that would take their place, with little more than a click of impossibly strong fingers, they morph into something so unworldly they may as well be a completely different species, which they pretty much are.

The thing about a vampire is that he or she is a cold-blooded killer. It's a choice, you see. There is no bloodlust coursing through your veins that forces you to feed off the blood of innocents, no drive you can't stop. It's a simple lifestyle choice for centuries before you become a true addict unable to turn away from an exposed neck.

Want to stay alive forever once you become infected? Then go and kill innocent people and suck their blood. That's the deal. It means they are pretty nasty people mostly, as they have chosen to live a life that means others lose theirs.

Not always evil, but you wouldn't take one to meet your grandma either, not if you liked her. Taavi rules them all in the UK, has strong European and worldwide ties—especially in Finland where he and his ancestors originate—and you do not mess with him. Ever.

The battle of the legs with the twins finished as we arrived at what I always think of as vampire headquarters. It's a sprawling place, set in large grounds constantly patrolled by vampires and dogs you really don't want to pet.

The sweeping, tree-lined drive is impressive and lulls you into a false sense of security and serenity, then you see the house. It's a jolt, even after you've seen it countless times. It's huge, ancient, and suitably spooky. There are a lot of vampires contained behind its walls, most of them so cruel and malevolent they make the ones that walk in the day seem like cute hamsters.

The building dates from the early sixteen hundreds, tall spires and dark stone, chosen specifically as Taavi likes to feel part of the old world, when vampire Heads all lived somewhere suitably intimidating so they could terrorize the villagers and have the virgins delivered with proper ceremony. He'd chosen well—one look at the place and you want to turn and run the other way.

As we got out of the car, I ignored the stares of the day militia, walked between the twins up the stone steps, and entered the gloom of the interior. My body itched and my tattoos squirmed at the vampire energy that permeated the air and would freeze your mind if you lost focus.

I was ushered into what I can only think of as Taavi's lair, and found myself stood in his rather over-the-top, and dark-as-his-heart reception room, black-etched windows making the space so dim it was almost impossible to see. But Taavi knew me, knew he didn't have to compromise, so kept it as dark as possible so he could stay awake even though it was daytime.

He is so old he has to rest when it's light, something to do with the sun and the energy it provides, although I've always suspected it's more to do with the hope it offers. Don't ask me how it works though, some vampire realities are strictly in-house. But he was weak as a kitten in the day, and half asleep.

I let my eyes sparkle darkly, the usual brown replaced by black with silver flecks, one of my many talents that allows me to see when others can't. Not Taavi, he would be looking at me as clear as if it was day. And he was royally pissed off.

I didn't blame him. After all, I'd screwed up in a way that could give him problems.

"You screwed up in a big way," said Taavi. See, told you.

"I know, I know. Look, Taavi, it wasn't my fault. You can't blame me for what happened. Someone did something to me. I just need time to find out who and what." I kept information to a minimum—people like Taavi rule by knowing more than the next in line.

"It is your job to stop this kind of thing from occurring, and now you are the one to expose us. How are you going to fix that?" Even after so long, Taavi still has a hint of an accent. On anyone else it would be endearing, on him it's strictly extra menacing.

"I'm going to deal with it, don't worry. I just need—"

"Time. Such a precious commodity for you humans. Something I normally pay little attention to, but it is of the essence at the moment, is it not? I am told that you are all over the news, on social media worldwide. Is this how an enforcer does his job? After all this time you are the one to show the world what we are capable of. What you humans are, anyway. Is it our time to come out of the shadows, Spark? Is that what this is about?"

"No, absolutely not," I said in a panic. This was bad. The last thing I wanted was the ruling vampire to think this was an open invitation to send his people out on the rampage and not care who knew.

"Enough. I am tired. Do you know I have not been awake at this time for over fifty years? Yet here I am, because of you." Taavi pointed a slender finger at me, like I didn't know who he was talking about. Man, this dude is scary. Even sat in the dark in his wingback chair, half crumpled and exhausted because of the time, he was as intimidating as hell.

He was like a praying mantis made of brittle paper. Skin sallow, pale like you wouldn't believe, but his power practically wiped your mind. Even in the depleted state he was in, his presence was enough to send you to the loony bin if you didn't put up careful blocks to stop his essence creeping into your skull.

"I'll deal with it. I need to find out what happened, who did this to me, and I need to see Rikka."

"You need to see me. I'm the one that found you first. You can see him when I say so. So tired." Taavi sighed and the room was silent.

I didn't speak, not a good idea, so I listened to the house and the creaks and groans of the ancient architecture, looked around the room like I'd done a few times before, admired the art and the old furniture, the books and the lush green carpet—it was seriously old skool, but then so was Taavi.

The silence stretched on and I wondered if he'd fallen asleep. I knew this was a struggle for him, and that meant he wasn't in the best of moods, but I was considering creeping out when he still hadn't spoken for five minutes.

"You may go. But you have until tomorrow, Spark, then I shall expect this to be put right. If not..."

"Sure, no problem. And, er, sorry for the trouble."

Yeah, I know, lame, right? Look, you try dealing with a sleepy but angry two thousand year old vampire after you've royally messed up and done the one thing you are supposed to stop happening. It makes you jumpy.

"Go away."

I went away.

"Oh, Spark, one more thing."

I knew it was too good to be true. The older the vampire, the more dramatic they seem to be. With my hand on the carved door handle, almost free of Taavi, I turned reluctantly, took a deep breath, and in my sweetest voice said, "Yes, Taavi."

"Oliver will accompany you."

"What!? You have got to be kidding." The room went not so much silent, as full of the quiet of Taavi's ancient anger. It was a real thing, visceral and frightening. You never argued with Taavi. You just didn't.

"Do you disobey me, Spark? You think because you are under the care of Rikka, Head of these pathetic Councils, that you may disobey me?" Taavi and all vampires paid little mind to the Councils, even though when it came down to it the Hidden Council could put them down if they so chose, but only with one hell of a war neither side wanted to even contemplate.

"No, Taavi, excuse me. It was just the shock. Anyone but Oliver though. He..." I gave up. He'd made up his mind. "Fine, but he better not try anything funny," I warned, trying to regain my manhood.

"He is under clear instruction to keep an eye on you, but he is not to interfere or misbehave in any way. If he does then he is on his own. I give you permission to stop him, or, haha, try." Taavi's laugh sounded as amused as a fly in a carnivorous Pitcher plant.

"As long as he behaves."

"Go away."

I went. And I actually got out of there that time.

A Sigh of Relief

Outside the room, I took a deep breath of air less tainted by the stench of decay and unholy age, set my eyes back to normal, and did a good job of holding back the sickness even from such minor use of magic. Bret and Bart were there, ready to take me into the city or home—yes, they know where I live. Everyone does.

Ours is a small world, and we all know too much about each other. In some ways it's like living in a tiny village where there's no privacy and everyone knows your business, but it's what has kept us under the radar. They frogmarched me out the front door, past more scary-ass vampires than is good for anyone's nerves. Taavi's Army of Ghouls, I like to call it, made up of the younger ones that can function in day as well as night.

His house is guarded so well it's ridiculous. He takes no chances and this was just the bit he let me see.

Deep underground in crypts would be hundreds, maybe thousands, of very old vampires, sleeping the day away. Some stay down there for years, decades, or longer, lost in their dreams of the past, conserving energy so they can arise for special occasions before sleeping through the centuries once more, catching up now and then and seeing what the future holds before retiring and taking another snapshot.

It's kind of appealing, being able to see how the future unfolds, like being a time traveler but with a lot of teeth and an unquenchable thirst for blood. And it is unquenchable at their age.

For regular vampires it's little but a choice, blood or fade away, for the older ones it grows into an addiction that is unbreakable, and then into something more—it becomes all they are. It's why they sleep. When they wake they will feed nearly constantly, probably like Taavi was right now.

The youngsters—and I say that relatively speaking—just revel in the health and vitality given them by the blood they steal, thriving on the blood magic that courses through their veins.

But, just like anyone who takes from the Empty, when they drink they are sick to their stomachs. The pain is unimaginable, I was once told. Like every nerve comes alive, screaming for release, and your blood, now tainted, burns so much many new vampires rip through their flesh to ease the fire within.

But they continue, do it anyway as it's part of the deal. It hurts like having your skin flayed and your exposed flesh soaked in vinegar, but you knock the clock back maybe another few months or years each time you take in that little bit of magic from the poor person laying at your feet, life over.

The older you get, the more brief the results. It's why the newly turned are so full of life no matter the age they were when infected, and the older ones are grumpy as hell and sleep so much. Just like everyone else, they need a way to escape their lives—the oblivion of sleep. Although I can't imagine what their dreams must be like.

I admit, I didn't know what to do. I had nothing to go on apart from a scrap of paper and the faint memory of a job I'd taken the day before. Now I had to go see Rikka, pray he didn't just kill me on the spot, and then deal with the mess.

I'm no Sherlock Holmes, in case you haven't guessed, but I had little choice. Plus, if I'm honest, I was anticipating a little vengeance. I'm not a violent man, but I was seriously looking forward to ripping someone's head off and maybe leaving the country.

Once we'd weaved our way through the dark corridors and rooms of Taavi's vast home, a vampire never out of sight, we finally made it back to the entrance. To fresh air, and if not sunlight, then at least not gloom.

Oliver was there, waiting, a smug smirk on his face that made you want to slap him and shake him and shout in his face, "What's wrong with you? Why do you do that?" You know the person I mean? He just has this look about him, this little sneer or smile always on his face that tells the world he's better than everyone else. In other words, the kind of face that needs to be hit. Hard.

Oliver is extra annoying as he is rather a handsome man—apart from the smackable sneer. For the first few centuries, certainly the first century or so, vampires pretty much remain as they were when first infected by another vampire. So you get all shapes, sizes, and ages.

This man was a pompous fool when reborn, and remains one to this day. I believe he is at least three hundred years old, although it's not information they often share, but he's kept his looks. A forty-year-old with shoulder length sandy hair, piercing blue eyes, high cheekbones, a straight nose, only let down by a weak chin that I know will break if punched. He's six feet, with an athletic build but weird square shoulders that make him look like a fit clothes hanger. The worst thing of all is that Taavi trusts him, uses him for a lot of business, and Oliver has strong control over the other vampires in Taavi's employ.

I say employ, but it's more protection than employment, although they certainly get paid, and well. Taavi is Head of the Vampire Council, the only Council where they actually have members, refusing the rest as they see it as beneath them or merely hate that they can't always get their own way. They do send representatives to the Hidden Council when told though. Nobody refuses such an order, not even vampires.

Taavi needs eyes and ears out in the world to maintain his position, and Oliver is often the man that runs it all. Today was my lucky day as he was strictly mine. What joy.

"Spark," said Oliver as he nodded and walked with me and the Chinese twins to the car.

"Oliver." I ignored him then, otherwise I'd say something that would get me into trouble. He smirked. Ugh.

Back in the car, the fight for a man's right to spread his legs wide, no matter the circumstances, resumed, but we soon arrived back where they'd picked me up and I was dropped off in the city center.

"How about a lift back to my place?"

The twins shook their blank heads in unison. Oliver turned around in the passenger seat and smiled at me. How I stopped myself from slapping him is testament to my emotional control. I stepped out into the drizzle. So did the creature known as Oliver.

I checked my watch—it was only ten in the morning. Man, I had a long day ahead of me.

Food. I needed food.

Time for Breakfast

If you ever happen to find yourself in Cardiff and are hungry, then there is only one place to go. Madge's Cafe. And that was exactly where I was headed. I think better on a full stomach as it dulls the pain and the sickness, and besides, I was ravenous.

I pulled my suit jacket tight against my shirt, huddled against the cold, and tried not to act like people much worse than the police were after me. Sticking to the alleys, I wound my way through town out to Splott, took turn after turn deep into student accommodation territory, and finally made it to Madge's on the outskirts of a small industrial estate.

Oliver trailed me the whole way like some kind of needy puppy, but he kept quiet, sullen and clearly unhappy about his orders for the day. I knew him though, knew he was waiting for me to slip up so he could take advantage and watch me unravel. No chance.

"You're going in there? Seriously?" The handsome coat hanger scowled at the battered sign and the steamed-up windows, the scuffed door and the peeling paint of a place I adored.

"Yup. You got a problem with that?"

"You have things to do," he said, almost like an order.

"And I'm doing them. I need to eat. We don't all live through the destruction of others, some of us just pay for our meals with cash, like normal people."

He sniffed and sneered. "Normal people," he spat.

"Yeah, you know, community spirit, keeping the old businesses alive, supporting the locals, all that." He stared at me blankly. "Whatever. Wait here, there's a good boy." Oliver's fists clenched and he bared his canines. I shrugged.

Opening the door to the cafe was like coming home, except I wouldn't dream of letting my sanctuary get dirty or smelly. The greasy, warm air hit me like a smack across the head with a loaf of moldy bread and I sighed, breathing easier for the first time since I came to my senses that morning.

Aromas of fried bread, bacon, eggs, tea and toast assaulted my nostrils and I probably gained a few pounds just inhaling the air. Aah, it's the small things in life.

The buzz of the cafe was more welcome than you can imagine, a little normality in a sea of strangeness. I couldn't believe it was still so early, and the cafe was packed.

As I stepped inside, a number of heads turned, and the room if not fell silent then certainly quietened down. Those that knew me stared open-mouthed, those that didn't, well, they carried on about their business, which mostly consisted of shoveling inexpensive, tasty food into their mouths, asking their eating companion how Madge managed to do it all so cheap, and groaning as their waistlines expanded and kept the city's fixer of snapped zips in brisk and regular business.

Madge was behind the counter, scowling at customers, wiping surfaces with a cloth probably as old as her, shouting over her shoulder for her poor kids to get a move on and stop messing around. She is a grumpy one and I love her for it.

Madge is sixty, going on four hundred, and has always looked the same. Thick spectacles, a mass of frizzy gray hair, deep frown lines, and the greasy apron I swear must be glued to her. She's a witch I guess, although she doesn't get involved in magic business or politics.

She likes to run her cafe, scream at her kids— poor things, they're still under the thumb and not one of the three of them is under two hundred—and practice her highly evolved art of utter contempt for all things sentient on her many customers. She also knows everything that goes on in the Hidden world, and I guess she is a mother figure to many of us—if your mom is a sourpuss and mostly ignores you and you like being insulted. Hey, you take what you can get, right? I know I do.

I squeezed past the mess of mismatched tables and chairs dotted haphazardly around the cramped room, smiled fondly at the sticky linoleum and the flock wallpaper dripping with the greasy residue of a million fry-ups, and tried to ignore the looks I got. It wasn't easy.

This was a mixed place, half full of students, factory workers, and truckers getting a cheap breakfast, half full of people from my world, and most weren't pleased to see me. Even less pleased than usual, as in my line of work some shrink at the sight of me as it means Rikka sent me and knows what they did.

Nodding at familiar faces, I got a few scowls in return, and decided to blank the lot of them.

I needed food, then I had work to do. I tried not to think about my impending visit with Mage Rikka— another Finnish dude. For some reason they have a monopoly on all things magic related.

The rumors go that Finland is where it all somehow started many thousands of years ago. Someone uncovered a way to unleash the Empty, and peel back the layers of the Hidden world, and things sort of spiraled from there. You know, the usual— unleashing the demons from hell scenario and magic pours forth into the world, and some dude managed to deal with them and then there you have it, magic is a thing. You can know it, own it. Become it.

Go to any country and those at the top of the food chain will be either direct descendants of ancient Finnish warriors or more usually hard-nosed aristocracy, or at least have some of that blood coursing through their veins.

Maybe it was the cold, maybe it was the seat of ancient powers that welled up there for some reason. I don't know, and at that moment I didn't care. I just wanted a cuppa and a big fry-up.

I watched some of the wizards, the half-dead, or the who-knows-if-they're-dead scroll through their tablets and phones, amazed I was still alive. None of them would look at me now I was close. There was no point hiding, it would only cause more trouble, so I may as well fill my belly before I continued with what would be a very long day. One I would hopefully stay alive to see the end of.

"Morning, Madge. Usual please, love. You're looking particularly radiant this fine morning."

"Your hair looks stupid," said Madge as she slammed a cup on the counter and splashed tea in from a metal teapot.

"You look divine." I winked, spooned two sugars in, then added a splash of milk. "Bring it over?"

"Don't I always?" Madge shouted orders to her kids and I took a seat at an empty chair. The two students already sat at the table continued their conversation, ignoring me. Perfect.

I was done for, shattered already and the day had just begun. I dared not close my eyes for fear of falling asleep, but I tried to piece together the night before and what had led me to do what I did. What a mess.

I had all of thirty seconds before I got a tap on the shoulder. I say tap, it was more like somebody dropping half a house onto a deltoid.

Here we go, I thought, knowing it wouldn't be someone wanting to say hello and wish me a pleasant day. I turned.

"You make mess. You make it bad. Your job stop this happening. You do opposite. Tree not like trouble. Tree want quiet life."

This was all I needed. I craned my neck and looked up, and up, and up, into the deeply furrowed face of Tree. It didn't look happy, not that it ever did. Mind you, the mini-mountain never looked sad or gave signs of any other emotion really. It didn't have the most expressive of features.

Tree is what you would call a troll. Actually, it is a troll, no doubt about it. You'd be surprised how many of them there are. You'd be surprised how many of everything there are. You know that thing I did earlier, the whole blending into the background so you don't notice me? Well, certain species have that kind of built in, like it comes with the package—lucky them.

As it's part of who they are, they don't have the sickness as part of their daily lives. Yes, they are using magic, but it's innate for certain things, like being able to blend in and stop Regulars seeing you as you really are. Their magic is what makes them, it's their essence, so no sickness. It's only humans that have to deal with that side of the equation.

Trolls, as you may have guessed, are not the most imaginative of fellows. You can't blame them for that though, they are made of rock after all, and the whole moving about at speeds faster than a glacier and talking thing is a very recent advancement.

These are ancient beings, like seriously old. There at the beginning of the world after everything settled down and rock was solid and mountains were real. They lived up high where the air is clear and oxygen levels are low, and they were alive but not alive. They hibernated, I guess you could call it.

Trolls never thought much of anything, just went about their troll business. Very slowly. But now and then one would turn up on lower levels, and the increased oxygen to their crystal brains sort of woke them up, to a very limited degree. They gave themselves names, like Rock, or Tree, or Boulder—the usual trollish stuff—and some found themselves managing to survive, sometimes even thrive, in the world of man and once-man.

So they had to adapt, and credit where credit's due, they did. Suffice to say, that you can't walk down the street looking like a seven, sometimes even nine foot troll, with a head made of rocks and a body like a mountain in an ill-fitting tracksuit and not draw attention to yourself.

But that's not what people see. When they look at Tree they see a big guy, overweight, in serious need of a fashion makeover, but just a regular bloke. Just as well, because if you were seeing what I was seeing you would be in no mood to eat your breakfast.

Let me give you a warning. If you see someone that just looks big, tall, or maybe with a rather square head and minimal facial expression then be nice to them. It hurts when they hit you. And if you see someone really tall, but slim like a basketball player, then be extra nice—they aren't trolls, and I'm not about to tell you what they are, but they make trolls seem real softies. It's why I don't watch the game. Too many bad memories.

"Leave me alone, Tree, I've had a bad morning." I slurped my tea, so thick you kind of half ate it, and pretended like the tablecloth was of interest.

My shoulder felt like it had turned to runny eggs, and not in a good way. "What you gonna do, eh?"

Man, I knew it was serious. This was the most I'd ever heard Tree say in... Well, ever! "I'll sort it. I just need to eat, to think. Don't worry." I kept my eyes down. Tree was easy to take offense if it saw the slightest hint of a smile, and I'm an optimistic kind of guy.

"Tree is worried. Tree not want trouble."

"I know, buddy, and I'm sorry, okay?" I lifted my gaze from the table and addressed the rest of the people in the room as many were now staring at me, waiting to see what happened. "Look, everyone, something happened to me, somebody did something to me, and I woke up and, well, you know the rest. But I'll deal with it. Have I ever let you down?"

There were murmurs of approval, and disapproval, but the fact was they all knew me, and knew I was very good at my job. I keep them safe; I keep them hidden. Nobody wants a war; nobody wants to be labeled a freak and hunted, and that was what would happen if Regulars knew about us. We just want to be left alone to beat the crap out of each other in private. You know, magic style.

The students were confused, the magic folk were in two minds about killing me or letting me be, and I was starving.

"Here you go, Spark, and sort that hair out." Madge plonked the plate down on the table, threw cutlery at me like she wanted to do me serious harm, handed me a bottle of ketchup that was so congealed at the lid I was sure it smiled at me, and retreated behind the counter.

"Thanks, Madge." I admired the plate of food. Two sausage, three bacon, three eggs, beans, hash brown, toast, black pudding. Bliss. I picked up the knife and fork, rolled my shoulder now it was minus one troll, and tucked in.

I didn't even get to dip my toast in runny egg.

"Spark, I'm gonna kill you."

Uh-oh.

No Eggs for Me

Toast poised mid-air over that golden goodness, I tried not to gulp and pushed my chair back. I stood, crunchy brown slice still in hand.

"What do you want, Dancer?" I asked, and no, he doesn't like to boogie. His skill involves much more co-ordination and subtlety, primarily bringing the dead back to life. A necromancer. He is also a mean bugger and has no friends. Dancer also works for my boss, on a much more regular basis than me.

I knew my breakfast was over. Time to go pay Rikka a visit; no avoiding it any longer.

"I should kill you right now," said Dancer, jabbing a finger into private airspace in front of my face, dirty fingernails stinking of soil and death—he'd obviously had a busy night digging up somebody for one reason or another.

"You can try," I sneered, trying to flex my bicep as I stood and squared to him, the effect slightly ruined by the toast dripping butter onto the linoleum.

Dancer stared at me, clearly trying to figure out what to do. He knew I wasn't to be messed with, that my looks were deceiving, but he also knew that the chances of anyone stepping up to help me out if he tried something were minimal—I wasn't Mr. Popular at the moment. He sighed. "Boss wants to see you. Now."

"Fine, just let me finish my—"

"Now! And what's with the ghoul outside? Making new friends, are we?"

I dunked my egg, took a bite of toast, and bowed to the watching misfits. "See you later, Madge." I waved at her as I goose-stepped after Dancer who was already at the door, holding it open for me and scowling through his thin and pale lips from a face I had thought about punching more times than I'd eaten at Madge's. And I eat there a lot.

"Sort out your hair," said Madge.

I stepped out into the cold; the door closed behind us.

Oompf. "Why you goddamn—" I felt his icy necromancer skills tug at my tendons and reacted instantly. My tattoos flared, eddying around me and swarming into the Empty, sucking what was needed out and into my right hand.

Feeling like Spiderman, I flipped my hand upright and blasted the tiniest sliver of dark magic toward Dancer, visible like a spiked line of noxious smoke so black it would freeze a Regular's heart. Not that they could see it now I was back to being myself. I'd just look like I was in need of my meds.

"Argh!"

"I told you not to mess with me, Dancer. What the hell?"

"My hand. You took my finger off!"

"I'll do a lot more than that if you try any of your animation tricks on me, Dancer." The idiot had tried to take me over, make me move against my will like he did his stinking corpses. What the hell was he thinking? All I did in return was fire a little of the dark stuff at his pinkie. Hardly a scratch really.

I kept the sickness out of my face. Dancer managed less well. His already waxy skin turned kind of yellow, like he was the corpse, and he fought to stay upright as the Empty came to take its payment.

Why he had bothered, I don't know. I was going, wasn't I? Guess he just thought he could try it on as I was in trouble already. His loss.

"My finger! Look at it," he moaned like a baby. I dunno, some people. It wasn't like he couldn't grow another one—a few weeks and he'd be right as rain. For a bloke that raises the dead for a living—and for fun, I have the sneaking suspicion—he sure was being dramatic.

"The new one will be nicer, all pink and shiny. You need a bit of color anyway." Dancer just stared at me with hate. "Well?"

"Well, what?"

"Where's the ride then? Look, if you dragged me out of Madge's just to play these games and Rikka didn't send you then I'll go back and finish my breakfast."

Dancer nodded down the street a little, past the bemused Oliver. There was no mistaking one of Rikka's vehicles. Right then I wished I had my own transport, but I could use one of Rikka's when I needed wheels, so I guessed I'd have to tag along with old pinkie.

I couldn't resist. "Hey, Dancer, guess what? I have a new nickname for you now. Pinkie, how does that sound? Kind of nice, right?" I gave him my most winning of smiles, but for some reason he wasn't impressed. "Suit yourself," I said, and walked away, ignoring Oliver.

"You coming?" I called over my shoulder. Dancer, a.k.a. Pinkie, clutched his hand and joined me at the SUV.

Rikka, Mage Rikka as he prefers to be called, actually insists—he thinks it makes him sound more intellectual than wizard—is a bit of a car buff, and he has a small fleet of identical vehicles his staff or part-time employees can use for his business. They are, to put it mildly, a little OTT for my taste. But I seldom drive and don't own a vehicle—this way fuel is free and I always have new car smell, which is awesome.

Cardiff is not exactly teeming with off-road opportunities, at least not in the city center, and anyway, you really don't want to get Rikka's vehicles dirty. Nevertheless, he runs a fleet of Range Rover Sport SUVs just because he likes room and comfort. Fair enough, as he really does need the room. You'll see, just wait until we meet him, okay? It's not like he goes out much though, but anyway, it is what it is. He likes gas guzzlers and can afford it.

"What, you not gonna open the door for me?" I asked Dancer.

"Just get in." He walked out into the road and opened the driver side door and clambered in, moaning about his finger and giving empty threats.

I joined him inside and put on my seatbelt. Safety first.

The rear door opened and we both turned.

"What the hell are you doing?" shouted Dancer, face as dark as his art.

"Don't think so, Oliver."

The vampire scowled at us and said, "Taavi said to watch you, Spark, until this is dealt with. All of it." He moved to get in and me and Dancer exchanged glances.

Dancer was ready to call up all manner of nasties and I had to put an arm on his shoulder. I stared into his eyes, shook my head.

I turned to Oliver, still half inside. "Look, you may have your orders, but I don't answer to you, or Taavi. Dancer certainly doesn't, and I know for a fact Rikka will go mad if you make his car smell of vampire. I'm going to his place now, make your own way. But get out of the damn car, right now!"

Oliver's eyes widened and I could see his mind weighing up the options. He got out and was gone.

He'd be there before us. Vampires can move fast, really fast.

"Okay, look, Dancer, I know I messed up, but I'm trying to fix it." He gave me a cold stare. "Fine. I was going to fix it. Nobody can think on an empty stomach though. I just needed breakfast. Look, I've already seen Taavi so I needed some down time."

"You've seen Taavi, already? Damn, Spark, you really are in trouble if that guy got you so soon. Even the Boss, um, Mage Rikka, only just heard. That's why you've got the vampire escort then?"

"Yeah. As for Rikka, it's because he insists on ignoring the TV and the Internet," I said, knowing how much the Boss hated what he called a "temporary blip on the road back to the good days."

Rikka still believes that the time of magic will come and we can all somehow live together, Regulars and Empties—what we sometimes refer to ourselves as.

He thinks that the new technology is a bad idea, aches for times long past, when he was a child and things were simpler.

"Whatever, but he's not happy. Far from it. You better tread carefully, you know what he's like when he's in a mood." Dancer turned to me. "How could you, Spark? How could you be so stupid? And you killed someone. You actually killed an innocent Regular. Are you nuts?"

Dancer isn't a bad guy, not really, just a bit full of himself. He may enjoy playing with dead dudes but he is no killer, and as far as I know has never killed a human being, vampire, troll—not that you can—or anyone you would class as a sentient being.

He's still a muppet though, but harmless. Unless you're dead and somebody paid him to re-animate you for reasons I try not to ever think about as otherwise I know I won't sleep well at night.

"It was an accident. I can't believe it either. Poor guy. Okay, let's get this over with. Take me to your leader." I know, lame right? It's just I've always wanted to say it and that was my chance.

"Dick." Dancer started up the Range Rover and pulled out into the damp streets of Cardiff.

I tried not to let my half finished breakfast come up. Yeah, Mage Rikka has that effect on you.

The Big Boss

Mage Rikka is the head honcho in the UK for all things magic related—he's even got a certificate and everything.

Although there are any number of subsets of people, and species, that have their own leaders or rulers, officially known as Heads—and some that answer to nobody and you couldn't organize them if you tried, have you ever met a troll?—we all ultimately answer to Rikka in our country.

He has an elevated position as not only UK Head of the Dark Council—nearly always composed of wizards as nobody else takes to rules and the Laws like they do—but also the UK Head of the Hidden Council.

The Hidden Council encompasses all Hidden, including vampires, whether they like it or not. Not that the vampires play by the rules, and you would never see Taavi doing something just because Rikka said so. It's all a bit daft really, as the Hidden Council beats the Dark Council—which is strictly for human magic users, so why they bother I don't know. That's humans for you, always got to have their own thing and make life more complicated.

All wizards, witches, users and abusers of the Empty that aren't innately magic by right of birth or species, a.k.a. humans, as well as those that are truly magical beings—true Hidden—answer to him. This is not an option. It is how it works for the Hidden. Think of it like normal humans answering to the law, except ours is written with a capital L, so it makes it more important—see how they think?

Rikka is our law, or "Law," and he dispenses justice or punishment as he sees fit. As long as he keeps everything in check then there is little interference from the Hidden or Dark Councils. Why we still insist on the "Dark" bit I don't know, I guess it stuck long ago, but there is no other magic for humans. It's all dark, and it all hurts to use, but I suppose other species don't have that problem, so for them it's just magic. Not even that, they just are what they are.

It's a strange hierarchy and not one that has any specific rules as to conduct, and that's probably why we get ourselves into trouble, and why there are people like me. More than anything else I'm an intermediary, able to move between Heads, species, Houses, Wards, loose collectives, even gangs, and usually be welcome.

What can I say? I'm an amenable kind of guy who deals with many problems that arise. I arrange meetings, truces, sometimes even fights when there is no other option, and basically enforce what Rikka wants.

He has his businesses, and he certainly has his people, but for the proper work, the delicate stuff, he calls on me and a few others. Semi-freelancers, more world-wise than many Hidden. People who know the lay of the land and can talk without blowing someone up, or conjuring a demon just because a zombie spilled your pint, or a necromancer stole that corpse you had your eye on.

Enforcer. Dealer of justice or punishment. Arbitrator, peace keeper, and all round lackey to the Boss.

Why the big wigs all chose Cardiff is a long story, but it goes back centuries and all stems from everyone failing to keep up with the changes of ever-advancing societies. Stuck in the middle of it all, in large cities like London, things easily got out of hand.

They couldn't cope with the pace, found no peace with things moving at breakneck speed, and as technology took jump after jump they all moved out here, where the pace of life is a little slower and there is room to breathe.

Personally, I think that is all nonsense and they just like the countryside—it's right on your doorstep here—and they are a shrewd lot too. You get a castle in Wales for the same price as a crappy apartment above a butcher's shop in Central London.

Anyway, whatever. I was being taken to meet my boss, and I felt sick. It had nothing to do with magic or a greasy breakfast either.

Did I mention I'm sort of a detective too, unofficially? No? Well, it comes with the territory. Enforcers need to track down the troublemakers, find solutions to seemingly insurmountable problems, and placate angry species or humans, which means doing a lot of detective work and knowing a lot of things. People too. Although I use people like this: "People." See me doing bunny ears?

Rikka keeps odd hours, meaning he never seems to sleep, or not in a bed anyway. Although, because of his size, I seriously doubt there is a bed massive enough for him, but with his money he could get one made, I'm sure. But I digress.

Dancer pulled up the SUV alongside several identical vehicles and we got out.

"Goddamn. Oliver again," I muttered. He was at the end of the row, looking as smug as ever.

"If Rikka sees him you'll be in even more trouble," said Dancer, smiling.

"Any more grinning and I'll tell Rikka you gave him a ride."

"You wouldn't dare!"

"Try me."

We ignored Oliver, knowing even he wasn't stupid enough to follow us inside House Rikka territory. The fact he was looking increasingly annoyed lifted my spirits a little, not enough to make me do a jig, but it helped.

I followed Dancer through the front of the building, past Rikka's heavies who stared at me blankly —trolls, they are very good at hanging around looking big and menacing, because they are—and tried to stay as cool and calm as a rapper named after a refreshing beverage, as I walked alongside Dancer past the reception. I winked at the new girl.

A few twists and turns later, through a private door you could never open without being one of us, and we were in Rikka's lair.

Guess where we are. No? It's a health club, a fitness center of all things. I know, right?

Of all the places Rikka could set up as his home turf, his seat of power, his place of business, he picked a leisure center. He thought it was brilliant. "Gotta love these recurring subscriptions," he told me once, rubbing fat hands together with glee. "It's the best business model in existence. People sign up for a year, pay in advance with no way of getting out of it, and then they hardly ever use the place. It's like printing money."

He runs a load of them, all over the country. Weird, but smart.

When people first meet him, they expect to be taken to a night club, some seedy joint, maybe with strippers and vampires or something, loads of weird stuff going on and all Gothic and scary like. Or something like Taavi's, proper old skool with skulls and ancient, forbidden books, maybe even a few lesser demons on leashes just in case, but no, they go to "Rikka's Fitness Emporium." That's what it's called! And he has loads of them, and people pay him a fortune for the pleasure of not getting fit. Some even use it just to have a shower and the odd sauna. Nuts. Whatever. Wish I'd thought of it.

Rikka set up shop in a large back room in a corner of a proper hardcore gym. There are no shiny machines here, this is members only. Rikka's people. And they are serious about their muscle. There is always more testosterone in the air, and more steroid use, than at Mr. Olympia. Some of these guys would win if they cared for such a title—they don't.

Rikka doesn't lift weights though, he lifts chocolate. And cakes, and ice-cream, and anything he can stuff into his mouth—if he can find it beneath the folds of fat that make him look like a partially deflated football with a lot of hair.

Dancer opened the door to the gym. The stench of sweat, the clanging of weights, and the grunts of the jacked greeted us.

I saw Rikka over in the corner. He had donuts left on his desk. I wished I'd still had memory loss as I caught sight of the jam-filled goodies. If you knew Rikka then you knew that was a very bad sign indeed.

Dancer closed the door behind us; everyone looked at me.

I wished I was back at Taavi's. At least vampires aren't as sweaty.

What's Your Plan?

I walked past the meat-heads, although many of them were trolls—so, rock-heads, I guess—plus a few dwarves up from the mines, or able to drag themselves away from their mountains of gold for a bit of business topside, and a few shifters.

The place was busy, as always. Serious Hidden lifters aren't fans of shiny chrome and the latest fashions, especially when they have to wait for Regulars to finish their sets, so Rikka's place is always rammed. Everyone can be themselves, and it's always a relief to not have to pretend to be something that you aren't. Which meant there was a group of eight foot tall—and almost as wide—trolls at the squat rack, a monstrous thing looking more like some arcane torture device than exercise equipment.

Rikka got the floor reinforced years ago after an accident, and upgraded the equipment to make it more specialized. The rack was modified for trolls, skip-loads of plates were delivered, bars thicker than a human leg were specially commissioned and the trolls were happy.

A few dwarves were doing curls. In place of the usual barbells and dumbbells were bespoke hammers, huge things that I couldn't even dream of lifting. But they were happily pumping out the reps, going up and down the rack. Man, they have some serious biceps. All that mining, I suppose.

There were a few mean looking goblins at the adapted shoulder press station, shouting and cursing at one another. All were sweaty and sick looking, as none of them would admit defeat and proclaim another stronger.

There were a few regular looking humans, although even then some of them were using equipment that was way too heavy for a normal person, mostly those that spent only part of their time in human form.

And then there were the shifters, sticking to their own kind, bears and wolves, a few others, all pointedly ignoring the other groups, trying to outdo each other and pretend they had no interest in what anyone or anything else was doing.

The atmosphere was electric. Loud, and full of grunts, groans, the occasional scream.

Rikka thrived amid the testosterone, probably as it made him happy that his people, or those he could call on when in need, were ensuring they were as ready for work, and as strong, as possible. It also meant he knew exactly where they were.

One gym-rat in particular caught my eye, like she always does.

"Hey, Plum," I said, trying to look all handsome and carefree, but feeling a little self-conscious about the size of my muscles when faced with some of the dudes, or dudesses—with trolls, dwarves, and creatures like imps you can never tell.

Plum finished her set of bench press as I paused in front of her. She sat up and wiped her forehead with a towel. You know you have it bad when you find sweat sexy. "Hey, Spark. You're in trouble, you know that, right?"

I nodded. "I know." God she is hot. Plum is the name, and gorgeous skin tone is the game. She is adorable. Perfect blue-black skin, and you guessed it, a panther shifter. Not that I've ever seen her in full shifter form. They're funny like that, the shifters. She is about as lithe and cat-like as it's possible to be and still look human, and whenever I see her I expect to see a tail. I wouldn't mind if I did.

In case you haven't guessed, then she is seriously out of my league. She's out of everyone's league. She is also one of the best enforcers out there, excluding yours truly, of course.

There's no racism, sexism, or speciesism in this world. Anyone can be an enforcer, you just have to have the right skill set. Plum has the skill set all right.

Sorry, that's pretty juvenile of me. I have the hots for her, okay? But she's a nice woman and I think very highly of her, so no offense meant. It's just that her body...

"He's waiting." Plum nodded toward Rikka and gave me a well-meaning smile. Aah, the pity of a beautiful woman—take what you can get, is my motto. Or it is now, anyway. Plum lay back on the bench, grabbed the bar and, with a grunt, continued benching her three hundred pounds—her warm-up not quite finished.

"Spark, get over here this minute. What the hell do you think you are doing?" barked Rikka, spitting donut all over his desk.

"Coming, Mage Rikka." I took one last look at Plum for luck, straightened my back, adjusted my jacket collar, and tried to stop my tattoos flaring up and making myself disappear into the floor. I walked across what felt like an infinity of rubber matting and tried to come up with a reason why Rikka shouldn't just kill me there and then—I had nothing.

"You broke the Law," he said, wasting no time.

"I know, but it wasn't me, Mage Rikka." Lame, right?

I glanced at the chess board and pieces on his desk, our game still only half over. It made me shudder. It was partly to blame for my current situation, after all.

"Did you, or did you not, beat a Grandmaster in five moves then send dark magic out of your hand and boil his blood and make his eyeballs pop and his heart explode and make the last few seconds of his life, after beating him at chess, his one true passion in life I might add, entirely horrific?" Rikka stuffed a whole donut into his mouth. He obviously felt better for getting that off his chest.

"Yes. And no," I added hurriedly.

"You broke the Law," he said again. "And your hair looks stupid. Take it off."

The Laws—wizards, and those involved in the magical realms, aren't known for their imagination when it comes to naming various aspects of our life and the rules we have—are pretty serious to our kind. Set in stone, you might say, and you do not break them. Ever. There aren't many, but they are not to be broken.

You don't let Regulars know of the existence of magic. You don't disobey your House Head, Ward Head, any Head above you. You don't interfere with other species' ways unless they break the Law of the Hidden. And you sure as hell don't do it so it gets on TV. There are more, but that was what I was currently concerned with.

"Somebody set me up. And, um, I can't take the hair off, it's, you know, attached." Rikka looked at me dubiously, but left it at that. Weird. "Look, I wanted to get this all straightened out before I came to see you. Somebody did this to me. You know me, you know I'd never kill a Regular. Heck, I don't kill anyone." Rikka gave me a "look." "Okay, hardly anyone. But whatever happened this morning, I'm not to blame."

"So somebody else killed that chess player did they? Somebody else is all over the news, and that damn Internet so I'm told. You've gone VIRAL! You were caught on camera, film, phone, however it works. You were SEEN! Using magic!" Rikka hates technology, and he sure as hell wasn't happy about me being "viral."

"Mage Rikka," formality is always best at such moments, "let me put it right. I can sort this. I just need a little time. Nobody will believe it by the time I'm finished, I promise."

"Spark, you know better than anyone that this cannot be left alone. I've already had Taavi's Chinese goons over here, and apparently you've already talked to him. Before me!" Rikka gave me a hard stare for that, his eyes full of magic he could unleash in an instant.

He and the vampires are not the best of buddies. I decided to keep silent about Oliver. "And you know that this cannot be allowed. You have broken the cardinal rule. You've shown us to the world. Do you know how bad this looks for me? Members of the Councils have already been sending all manner of people here to find out what's going on, and some of them have been less than pleasant."

I could only imagine. Rikka may be our Head, but he isn't the worldwide leader of either of the Councils. There are a lot of countries and a lot of mages. He's one among many, but that didn't help me. If anything, it made it worse, as he had to show he dealt with his House in the correct manner. That meant dealing with me. Not good. Politics, politics, it's the same for us as it is for you. Drives you nuts.

"Eh, sorry. I was miles away." I'd lost focus, which was stupid.

"Christ, Spark, what am I going to do with you?"

"Give me a raise?"

Rikka glared at me, then pointed at Dancer and said, "What happened to your finger?" Dancer looked at his missing digit and I noticed the little pink stub that was already growing back. He was forcing the issue a little and was probably why he looked so sick, but that was his business.

"Lost it," he mumbled.

"You lost your finger?" Rikka was in no mood for sour necromancers.

"Yes. Sorry."

"Whatever. You guys are killing me, you know that? You are making me look bad, Spark. I will not stand for it!" Rikka's massive fist slammed into the desk, making the donuts bounce and the chess pieces almost topple. The shock reverberated up his arm and I watched, mesmerized, as his chubby cheeks wobbled like two silicone implants.

"Give me a little time and I will put this right, I promise. It's not like it hasn't happened before."

"Yes, but that was before TV and cameras, and this damn Internet. It didn't matter then, it was easy to cover up. Time is one thing you do not have, Spark. You are out of time, you should know that. I've got imps and trolls and seers and vampires and who knows who or what else to deal with, and none of them are happy. Not to mention the other members of the Councils. What the hell did you think you were doing?"

"That's it, Boss, I didn't even know my name. I didn't know who I was or where I was or what I was doing. Somebody did this to me. Give me a break, please?" I was desperate. He could put me down and not even skip a beat of his fat-lined heart.

"Okay, Spark, one chance, and one chance only. You have until tomorrow morning. Seven AM, that's when you did it, right? Seven this morning?" I nodded. "You have until then as that's how long I've been given to wipe this from the collective memory of the planet. Do you know what you've started? People, and, er, non-people,"—told you we had an issue with what to call ourselves—"are already clamoring for this to be the beginning of the New Order. If we are to keep them in check you need to deal with this."

"Thanks, Mage Rikka. I won't let you down."

"You already have."

"Did you send me on a job yesterday? I had this slip in my pocket, a receipt, and I wondered if this is what it's all about. Did you send me to see someone? Maybe that's the answer?"

Rikka stared at me in that scary way of his, his fat face morphing and contorting as he bored into my soul and I felt the sickness rise as the Empty flowed into him. He is so powerful it hardly touched him, but rather contaminated those around him instead.

He mumbled, then waved a hand over the chess board, our game and connection to each other over all these years now forever tarnished.

A tiny person danced around on the squares. She was a brown-haired woman, rather nondescript, but even in miniature she had eyes that would devour your very soul and you'd ask for more. She was twirling and shouting, carefree and wild, spinning and totally in the zone.

"You were supposed to deal with her. Ring any bells?"

It didn't. I shook my head.

The image vanished and I felt a little emptier inside. "You don't remember?" Rikka leaned forward. It was then I knew things were really serious. "You were supposed to deal with her. Don't tell me you haven't?" He actually looked panicked.

"Who is she?"

Rikka beckoned me closer with a sausage finger. I got right up to his bloated, sugar-coated lips and he whispered, "Ankine Luisi."

Oh no, I hadn't realized it was this awful. "The Armenian!?"

"Of course, the Armenian!" Rikka put a hand to his mouth after he realized he'd almost shouted.

This was bad. Real, real bad. The Armenian? Ankine Luisi? Damn! "What did she do? Why was I sent after her?" My stomach knotted like I'd licked a goblin's toes.

"Why do you think?"

I watched, transfixed, as sugar dropped from Rikka's lips onto his chin.

"She didn't, did she?"

"She did." Rikka nodded.

"What? The 'thing?' Really?"

"Yup. And you were meant to deal with it. Guess she wasn't too happy about that."

"That's out of our remit though, isn't it? She's, you know, the Armenian. It's their business to rein her in."

"She's here, so we deal with her if she breaks the rules. And anyway, I got the go-ahead from the Armenian Dark Council, who were ordered by the Worldwide Council."

"I bet they'll all be glad to see the back of her."

"So would I. You blew it, Spark. Now you need to put this right."

I sighed, tried not to show how little I was looking forward to this. "I will, you can count on me."

Rikka leaned back, seemingly satisfied. Voice back to normal he said, "Until seven tomorrow, Spark, not a moment later. Or else."

"No problem." It was the opposite. I was screwed.

I turned; the room was silent. All eyes were on me as I walked across the endless floor of the gym. I was so dazed I didn't even drool over Plum. That's how much the words "the Armenian" had stressed me out.

Ankine Luisi! Damn! I was screwed. Did I say that already?

"Oh, Spark?" I turned back to face Rikka. What now?

"I mean it. You know what will happen if you don't put this right? You're lucky I've given you this long. Anyone else and..." Rikka sliced a fat finger across the place his throat would be if he had a neck.

"I know. Don't worry."

"I'm not, but you should be."

I was gonna die. Horribly.

Just before the door closed, I popped my head back around. "Um, can I have a car, or a ride?"

Rikka looked up from some papers. "You know where the keys are, now get out of my sight."

This time I managed a quick wink at Plum. She ignored me. She was deep into new poundage territory.

Time for a Ride

Back at reception, I asked the new girl for a key and after a little to-and-fro, with a few winning smiles from yours truly that she almost seemed immune to, she gave me a set. I headed to the private parking area for Rikka's fleet of vehicles and pressed the unlock button on the fob then got in the Range Rover that flashed its welcome.

Oliver was nowhere to be seen, so things were looking up already.

The interior was nice. Quiet, with that new car smell that always makes you feel rich, even if it isn't your car.

What a mess. I was in this deeper than I could have possibly imagined and it would only get worse now I'd found out exactly why I'd done what I'd done.

Ankine Luisi. The Armenian. Your worst nightmare come true. And I'd been sent to deal with her. No wonder I couldn't remember what the hell had happened. She was one seriously scary lady, with some serious skills under the strangely plain exterior.

In movies, the vampires and the female antagonists are always all hot and sparkle. They get up with full make-up on and are always beautiful and shiny, but life isn't like that. Most people from our world are just everyday looking folks, apart from the odd extremely handsome man, of course. Ahem.

We look like you, like everyone else. Fat, thin, ugly, pretty, super hot, or super gross.

Those that weren't human at some time, or still human, are a different matter. The only way they can get along in the human world is to have some kind of screen up. It comes with the territory; it's just how it works. That's magic for you. It wants to stay hidden. In fact, it doesn't want to be here at all. That's why it makes you so sick to use it.

But for genuinely magical beings like trolls, goblins, dwarves, the proper, magical dwarves, and all the rest, then they have a natural filter that hides their true selves when in the company of Regulars. But they can't choose it. So, just like us, some look good, others are a mess, and there's nothing they can do about it.

The Armenian is different. She can take on many forms as that is her nature, what she is. If you meet her, and pray you don't, you would see a rather unnoteworthy looking woman of indeterminate age, maybe early thirties, maybe late twenties, with mousy brown hair, brown eyes, and rather plain features. That's her secret, her power, how she traps you.

But look closely, really look, and you find she has this "thing" to her, something that sucks you in, like a spider drawing you deeper into its web, and you are very lucky if you can ever escape.

Succubus, in other words. A siren, a truly, honest-to-goodness, other-worldly being that simply will not be tamed. She's wild, unruly, unmanageable, and dangerous as hell. The Armenians were as happy as an elf with a park full of children to steal when she decided to come play with us here in the UK.

What's worse was now it seemed she was in Cardiff and I'd been tasked with dealing with her once and for all. I didn't need to ask why, everyone knew. She was a wildcat, would answer to no-one, and had to be stopped. Rikka had finally been told that she had to go, and that had been passed on to me. As you can tell, I wasn't doing a great job of it so far.

Thud, thud, thud.

The bang on the window scared me nearly half to death and sickness blanked my mind as the Empty surged through my veins, instincts primed to fight in an instant.

"Bloody Oliver," I moaned, then turned.

Nope. It was Barrack, one of the goons from the gym, and a real pain in the ass. I sighed. The window wound down with a press of a button.

"What do you want, Barrack? I'm busy."

"You broke the Law, Spark, you gotta pay."

I was amazed I'd lasted so long without someone trying to beat the magic out of me, so it was kind of a relief. It made life a bit more normal. I dealt with this every day, his type of attitude and posing.

Let me tell you one thing now, and I've learned it from experience so it is definitely true. It doesn't matter how big they are, the little guy can always win. He just needs to be smarter, or faster. Well, I was faster than Barrack, and definitely smarter. Heck, his dumbbells were smarter than him.

Actually feeling relieved to have a distraction, and a way to release some nervous energy, I stepped out of the car. Barrack took a few paces back to let me out.

"Look, mate, I'm seriously not in the mood. If you want to go at it, then fine, but the Boss won't be happy if I can't deal with the current situation." I knew he wasn't listening. He wanted to fight. Whatever.

"I've never liked you, Spark. You and your stupid suits, and what's with the hair? You look like a mop."

"Ooh, scathing. You been thinking that one up the whole time I was in the gym?" By the look on his face he had, and it was the best he could come up with.

"Shut your face, you, you, stupid wizard."

"That hurts, Barrack, that really does." This guy is such an idiot. He's what you would call a genuine goon, used to do the less than savory work all mages in Rikka's position have to deal with when they are trying to run a business and also run a rather unruly magical menagerie.

Barrack lunged for me, huge body rippling with muscle like he'd been force-fed steak and steroids for years. If he got me in that bear hug I'd disappear into the slabs of meat like a gnat. He wasn't just big, he was freaky huge, looking even more so outside with his training vest and shorts on—a true freak of nature.

He is also a shifter, and it didn't take a genius to take one look at his monstrous frame, bushy beard, and coarse hair all over his arms and chest to guess what he shifted into. At least for me anyway. Even dopes like Barrack manage to control themselves in public places, so if a Regular was watching all they would see were two mismatched guys fighting.

His features rippled and the grizzly bear's teeth snapped at my head as the now seven foot beast tried to wrap huge, hairy arms around me and throttle the life out of me. Claws that would rip through flesh like butter were bent, ready to rip me to slices of raw protein, and you could bet he'd eat me in his current state.

Blackness enveloped me. I felt my eyes turn dark and flecked with silver, as my right arm shot up, heel of my hand punching out with the power of the Empty behind it and I connected with the wet, squishy nose of the bear-man. No point using much magic on the idiot, it wasn't needed.

He howled like a baby and the shifter shrank, replaced with a goon clutching his broken nose, tears streaming down his face.

"You bwoke my dose," he moaned as I opened the car door and settled myself again. Aah, new car smell.

"That's what you get for being such a muppet," I said before slamming the door. I started the SUV and was gone before he managed to set his mangled nose back into place.

Barrack isn't a bad guy, just dumb. A good goon. But I'm not an enforcer for nothing. We are quite good at what we do. The sickness passed as my tattoos settled down and my eyes became my own. I turned on the headlights as the rain came down again. Bloody rain, it's like summer was in denial—it always is in Cardiff.

As I drove, a plan formed in my mind. It was stupid, dangerous, could go badly wrong, but I had no other options or ideas. And besides, if I didn't sort out this magic faux-pas soon it wouldn't matter if I dealt with the Armenian or not. I would still be the most hated man in magic-land, so I had to put it right.

I pulled out my phone and dialed the last person I wanted to speak to: Dancer.

"What?" he said as way of answering.

"Fancy doing me a favor?"

"What do you think?"

"Okay, let me rephrase. How would you like to earn a favor in return from me?"

"Make it two. I do this, and you owe me two favors. No debate."

I thought it over. I had no choice. "Fine. Meet me at your favorite place."

"Be there in half an hour," said Dancer, the excitement in his voice clear.

"Make it an hour." I snapped the lid closed and headed to meet a vampire.

My Favorite Vampire

Favors in our world are different than in the Regular world. They don't come with questions or limitations. I'd signed my life away with Dancer by offering two favors. He could ask me anytime for pretty much anything in return, as long as it didn't break our rules.

Still, I could see little alternative and that was in the future, not now. Now was what I was worried about.

The dumb bear had given me a moment of clarity as the magic welled up. I'd let it flow for a moment and I suddenly knew what I had to do to solve the problem of the magic show I'd given that morning. I had to make it a lie. I had to undo it.

How?

I had to convince the world that what they'd seen wasn't true. That there was no magic in the world and the Grandmaster had not been killed, and that everything was hunky dory—carry on as normal please, nothing to see here.

First things first. Stop off at Kate's, then meet Dancer at the morgue. Easy peasy, lemon squeezy. Yeah, right.

Driving through the congested streets of Cardiff, it was clear that the circus I had created was just getting worse. There were TV vans everywhere you looked, all trying to get a scoop on the death of the Grandmaster and make it to the park where it had happened. What a nightmare.

It wasn't just the TV crews and the police though, and traffic was heavier than on match day at the Millennium Stadium. It was pandemonium.

People couldn't stay away from such things. They wanted to be a part of it, gape at the scene of the crime even though there would be nothing there now. The body would be gone, I was sure, or it would be in an hour or so by my reckoning. Plenty of time for me to have a chat with Kate then meet Dancer.

Okay, my plan was stupid, but I'm an enforcer, not a miracle maker.

*

I made it to Kate's in half an hour, and trust me, it should not have taken that long. Cardiff is small, and there aren't many routes you can take to get somewhere, but still. I hate traffic, it's one of the reasons

I usually enjoy this small city so much—apart from match days it's a breeze to travel around.

Kate lives in one of the converted dockland buildings. A huge red brick structure the developers didn't actually ruin when the city underwent a major overhaul. She has a nice spacious apartment she keeps in a condition that would make any estate agent proud —some would call her fussy, I'd call it having respect for where you live.

Anyway, I knocked on Kate's apartment door, then knocked some more, then some more. After five minutes she finally opened the door on the latch and peered at me, bleary eyed.

"Did you bring coffee?"

"Um, no. Sorry. I'm kind of preoccupied." I should have brought it. I wanted a favor, after all.

Kate peered at me with sleepy eyes, as if deciding if I was worth letting in sans caffeine, then slammed the door and removed the chain. She left it open a crack and wandered back down the hall into her kitchen.

I entered, and tried not to gape at the sight of her scratching at her well-rounded backside in just a pair of panties. I'd have to tell her to put something over her sleep attire, as the sight of women in panties and vest, all tussled and wild looking after sleep, does nothing for my concentration. Especially when it's Kate.

She padded barefoot ahead of me across an immaculate floor, like it had just been laid, and I tried to stay focused on the gloss of the wood rather than the shine of her skin.

In the kitchen, she yawned then flicked on the kettle. Continuing to ignore me, she got out two cups and spooned instant into them both. I got the milk from the well-stocked and orderly fridge.

"Have a nice sleep?" I asked, not wanting to get too serious too quickly.

"I was. Until someone woke me up," she accused.

"Sorry. You know I wouldn't call this early unless it was important." It was gone eleven, but Kate doesn't keep regular hours.

She's a night person. She's a vampire. A new one. Three years old, and I like her. A lot. Too much. So much it hurts. She is also smart as hell and has a way with technology, and that was why I needed her. One of the reasons, anyway.

Me and Kate go back, since very early on after her new life began, and we are good friends. As good as you can get when one of you fancies the other and the other has to resist tearing out your throat and gorging on your blood as you lie on the floor dying, terrified, wondering what the hell went wrong. Hey, what friendship is perfect, right?

You may think it strange that a vampire is making coffee and acting like a normal person, if rather late to rise, but what did you expect? Kate is a modern girl and lives in the world rather easily. She just has to suck the blood of humans now and then.

She eats, drinks, can use mirrors, doesn't disappear if you take her photo, and is fresh enough to the vampire scene to still be mostly untainted and even have nearly all her humanity intact. Most, not all. Unfortunately, it doesn't work like that. She is, to put it bluntly, no longer quite human.

But neither am I. I haven't been for so long I don't even know what that means now. I think I even miss it, being normal, but I'm not sure, and thinking about it makes me sad anyway.

There have been changes. Even in the few years I've known her she is different. A little colder, slightly detached and distant sometimes, but it will be a long time before she becomes truly unknowable and a different species entirely. She still has her humanity, and is doing her best to keep it.

Sometimes I wonder if this is why she insists on her apartment being so clean and tidy—her way of holding on to what she knows is a past life—or maybe her new state has made her slightly more obsessive. I've seen it happen before. New vampires get some strange quirks, and interests or tendencies become all-consuming. Better to take it out on the furniture and the kitchen counters than the world at large—that only leads to trouble.

We met because I dealt with her maker, something I don't normally ever get involved in, but it was a nasty business for all concerned. The guy was a loose cannon, not respecting the rules of our world or the vampires', and in a rare moment of mutual cooperation both the Dark Council and the Vampire Council agreed that the man had to go.

Yours truly was sent to deal with him, accompanied by several vampire enforcers, and let's just say that the guy is no longer with us and leave it at that, okay?

It was just a shame we arrived when we did. Kate was already bitten, almost gone, and even now I wonder if saving her was the right thing or not. I'm not sure she knows, either.

Kate had been totally freaked about her new life, went through all the pains and terrors that all have to come to terms with when turned. Some can't, and end it all, while others accept it, and quite a number embrace or even revel in it. Kate acknowledged it as an inconvenience and got on with her life.

She is part of our world now, and after I'd helped deal with her maker, we hit it off.

"Here. I like the hair. Bit drastic though, isn't it?" Kate put a mug in front of me as I took a seat at the kitchen bar, then put hers down.

"Thanks. And sorry for waking you. As for the hair, well, I, um, I messed up."

Kate lifted a perfect eyebrow. "So what's new?"

"No, I mean I really messed up." I put a hand up before she could talk. "But it's not my fault, honest. Apparently I was sent to deal with the Armenian and —"

"Ankine Luisi? Seriously?" Kate stopped with mug mid-air, then gulped steaming coffee fast, trying to kickstart the day.

"Yeah," I said glumly. "But it didn't go according to plan. I don't even remember yet, as the effects haven't worn off, but she did me over good and I am in deep trouble. I've already seen Taavi, and Rikka, not to mention a few other people I could have done without the pleasure of. I need you to help me out."

"With dealing with her?" Kate looked freaked.

"No. No, of course not. I'll deal with her later, maybe. But I need you to... It's best if I show you. Have you got your laptop?"

"Hang on." Kate jumped down and I tried, and failed, to ignore the jiggle under her vest, so turned back to my coffee as she wandered into the bedroom. I looked up and stared out of the floor to ceiling window that overlooked the bay—the view little more than gray cloud and gray water as usual—and watched the seagulls battle with the rain and wind.

Thankfully, Kate soon emerged, wearing jeans and a smartly tailored green blouse. She had her laptop tucked under her arm, so I could at least try to focus on saving my own skin for a while, rather than focus on hers.

Hot women suck, in some cases literally.

"May I?" I nodded at the laptop.

"Sure." Kate slid it across the counter and I flipped it open. I went to YouTube, got up the morning news clips—man, the view counts were nuts—and pressed play.

*

"Faz,"—she's the only one that calls me Faz, apart from Grandma, and I don't even mind—"what the hell? They'll kill you for this. It could start a war, or worse. It could mean the end of everything."

"Tell me about it. Look, things like this have happened before, more often than you would think, especially with every bloody move you make being recorded or photographed by some dude with a smart phone, but yeah, this is a bad one. That's why I need your help. Everyone's overreacting, but I guess this is the best footage ever of someone using magic. I was lost to myself. My usual defenses weren't up, so it was actually seen. You still, you know, working?"

"Of course I'm still working. What do you think I'd be doing?"

"Oh, I don't know. Hunting and killing human beings maybe. Hanging with vampires and bathing in blood. Nice orgies, that kind of thing." Yes, I'm an idiot, and yes, I knew as soon as I'd said it that it wasn't the best way to get a friend to help me out of a very bad situation. What can I tell you? I'm dumb now and then.

"If you're going be like that then—"

"I'm sorry, okay? Please, my mouth isn't connected to my brain at times. I'm an idiot."

"We both know that."

"Sorry. So, you are still working?" Kate just stared at me. "Okay, then how about you..."

Conspiracies

"Can you do that?" I asked, after I'd explained what I was after.

"Um, sure, piece of cake. Just for this guy though? That's rather limited if you ask me. Why not go all out? That way it's got a much better chance of being convincing. It's a backup, makes the whole thing seem genuine. I can go international if you'd like?"

"I love you. Not just a pretty face." Before I knew what I was doing I leaned over the counter and planted a wet one right on her cheek.

Eek.

There was silence, and it was a little awkward. Look, I didn't mean it like that. You know, that I love her, although I probably do. I meant, wow, thanks, that's great, you're a true friend and I owe you, that sort of thing. So, me being me, I thought I'd better explain that.

"Um, you know, as a friend and all. I love you like a friend and that is a great idea and, er, thanks."

Kate stared at me funny. If I wasn't so insecure deep down under the bravado then I could have almost hoped she liked the kiss and what I said. But I am, and I did hope. But I didn't dare ask, or try anything, as I valued our friendship. I knew from way too much past experience that me getting the wrong impression is more often than not what I mistake for come-to-bed eyes when really it's don't-you-dare-touch-me eyes, or I-love-you-like-a-brother eyes. Then I'm screwed, and alone. Again.

"Why do you do that?" Kate asked, shaking her straight, perpetual summer-blond hair away from her face.

"Do what?"

"Always have to crack a joke and never talk about things properly?" This was serious. She rested her lovely chin in her hands and stared at me with big blue eyes that saw every sad thing that welled up inside of me and screamed for release.

"Because I'm a fool and don't understand women. Because I'm scared of commitment, loss, love, and loneliness, and the only thing worse than not trying to find love is being rejected when you think you've found it."

Kate was taken aback. Told you I had a sensitive side. "Oh."

"So, are we good? Can you get onto this, like now? How long will it take?" For the first time since I came to my senses I had a glimmer of hope. I might pull this off and come out of it with my head still attached to my shoulders. Maybe.

"Give me two hours and I'll be done."

"What! Seriously?"

"I can do it in an hour if you really want it rushed."

"No, two is fine. I meant I'm amazed you can do it that quick. Genius."

"Not just a pretty face, right?"

"Absolutely."

Kate got up and walked around the counter, just stood there, looking all amazing and scary as hell too. Yes, scary. It's an issue, the whole vampire thing. Not enough to stop me hoping, but there's no getting away from it. Vampires are intense.

It's the hint of the ageless, this thing inside of them you know is there. It will creep up on them over the years, strip them of their humanity and there is no way to stop it. I've never met a truly old vampire, I mean truly old, that isn't cold and heartless.

Still, she is hot. And nice. Perfect, really. Okay, almost.

I got uncomfortable with her standing next to me while I was on the stool trying to finish my coffee so I jumped down. She stood on tiptoe and kissed me, right on the lips. It felt like magic. A kind I'd never experienced before. The familiar tingle but with no sickness—the opposite. All warm and wet, like love had been poured into my mind and I would do anything for this woman. Anything.

She stepped back and said, "See ya, then. I'll get right on it. I'll give you a call when it's done, okay?" Kate looked at me quizzically, head cocked to one side. Her lips glistened and I couldn't focus on anything else.

"Um, okay. Bye." I walked out in a daze, not knowing if the kiss was, you know, a kiss, or just Kate being Kate. Maybe one day I'll ask. Maybe not.

I stood the other side of the door and heard the chain go on. I almost felt like doing one of those soppy things where you put your hand onto the door and hope the other person is doing the same thing the other side. But I'm a dark magic enforcer. I rip the magic out of dangerous miscreants and leave them to cope alone. I know the true horror of humanity and it's worse than any devil I've ever encountered. I've battled vampires and I've blasted witches' eyeballs until they fizzed and popped, but I still almost did it.

I licked my lips; they tasted of her. They tasted of hope.

I walked away, wondering if Kate had a hand on her door. I'll never know.

Time to go to the morgue.

The Perfect Job

"I knew you'd call," said a smug Dancer as he met me on the steps outside the hospital—as with all good morgues, it was in the basement. I hate it when people are smug, unless it's me doing the smugging—that's a word, right? It is now.

"How?" I asked suspiciously.

"Stands to reason," he said with a smile that was making me have serious second thoughts about anything but slapping him, hard.

But I was limited as to options, and I wasn't exactly on talking terms with most necromancers. I didn't want to be with this one either, as they freak me out. "Is that right?"

"Yes. There's only one way out of this mess, and part of that is you needing my specialty."

Maybe he wasn't as stupid as he seemed. Maybe. "Okay, fine. Are you in then?"

Dancer wiggled his stub of a pinkie. It looked sore as hell. The little sprouting nub of a finger was red raw but already longer than earlier. He would pay for forcing things so soon, but that's necromancers for you —always messing with things they shouldn't be.

I tried to hide a shudder and steeled myself. "I'm sorry. Apologies for your finger. It won't happen again. And I would truly appreciate your help." I felt degraded saying it, but I needed him.

"Okay, I accept. Don't forget, you owe me twice for this. And I will collect."

"I know you will. Come on, let's get this over with."

Dancer smiled; I followed him inside.

*

One bonus of being in contact with the Empty is that you don't have to worry about signing in, paying for things, or freaking out about CCTV. Once you've done your apprenticeship—although it isn't made up of studying books and practicing on frogs, I can tell you that much—then you always have that little bit of magic bubbling away just below the surface.

It's part of you, a disguise like for the true Hidden, and normally it masks any magic use from Regular eyes. You know, apart from when you've had a run-in with a succubus. She must have worked me over good to have made my actions visible to all.

The magic that is always with you isn't enough to make you sick, or put a downer on your day-to-day life, just sufficient to allow you to blend into the background so people don't notice you unless you act like an idiot—like I did earlier on and then freaked and dyed my hair.

It's why so many involved in magic are what you would call unsavory elements. Or, to put it bluntly, criminals.

Imagine if you could walk into a bank, a nice jewelers, or a technology store and pick up what you wanted and walk out. Tempting, right? It's not just about magic either, it's the knowledge that it's there if you need it.

All the best thieves are the ones that hide in plain sight. The everyman. The person with enough confidence to walk into a place, pick up a 50" TV and just wander right on out like they have every right to.

Or the person who puts on a suit and a name tag, walks into a jewelers and starts writing on a clipboard and asking questions, and in minutes has the staff running into the back to get the books and call their boss while he walks out with a million in watches.

It's all about attitude. Add to that the ability to not be seen—you're there but not there—and it's easy to see why anyone who has touched that infinite and dangerous place becomes somewhat addicted to the rush and the power it gives.

Why am I telling you this? Just so you know that we didn't have to sign in, we didn't worry about CCTV, and we were perfectly relaxed as we pushed through the doors into the morgue after Stanley buzzed us into his place of work.

Now I was back to being me, and no longer seriously depleted from the terrible events of the morning, I hid in plain sight and had no need for a disguise. Lesson learned? Lie low. Don't panic, dye your hair, and cut it off in a tizz like a little kid.

"I guess I don't need to ask what you guys want," said Stanley before he turned back to the cadaver on the slab, scooped out a liver then plopped it onto a scales with a squelch. He licked his lips. I swear, he does it every time. He can't get enough of this kind of thing. "I must say, I'm surprised to see you two together. Not usually a team, are you?"

"Desperate times," I said, feeling weird as I was an Alone. I never worked with anyone else, and certainly not people like Dancer.

"Blondie here got himself into a mess and I'm helping him clear it up," said Dancer, smiling that thin-lipped smile of his that always makes me want to smack him across the head with something heavy and pull off his lips with a pair of rusty pliers.

"I heard." Stanley turned and looked at us both in that unnerving way of his—it gives you the creeps. "I like the hair. Suits you."

"Thanks." I put a hand through the hacked locks. It still felt weird, like I was missing half my head.

"So, what can I do for you fellas?" Stanley smiled, like he didn't already know the answer.

I hated it, hated it more than anything. Even just being in his presence makes you feel about as important as an ant. It's his smile, the twinkle in his eyes, the knowing nod and the sheer futility of it all.

Stanley is a seer, and not just any old seer. Stanley is what they called a nutter. Haha, joke, sort of. Stanley can not only see the future, he's stepped over the line, and there is never any going back. It's why, out of all the possible paths you can choose when you open yourself to the Empty, looking into the future is the worst possible choice you can make.

Go too far, which is easy to do, especially before you have decades of practice and know exactly what you are doing, and you're stuck with the lot. Yeah, all of it.

That's why there aren't many seers, not real ones. Most of them kill themselves because they push the limits and can't handle what they unlock. Stanley seems to enjoy it though, and that's what makes him so damn freaky and frightening.

I could see Dancer squirming and shifting from one leg to the other. He knew as well as I did that our whole being there was pointless and nothing but a little amusement for Stanley. Déjà vu of the worst kind, as he really had already seen it happen. More. He'd genuinely lived it, experienced every aspect of his own life until death, and he isn't phased in the slightest.

It amuses him. There's nothing scarier than that.

So there we are, a necromancer and a dark magic enforcer, feeling like bugs as we stood staring at a smiling seer with a heart now in his hands and a faraway look in his eyes. He is always well dressed underneath his lab coat, is well fed, gets regular exercise, and looks like a white collar banker rather than a guy who spends his days up to the elbows in other people's goopy insides, living a life already lived.

People. Nothing weirder, right?

We snapped back to attention, both of us clearly thinking about the strange life of Stanley. "Um, can we borrow the chess player for a bit? Please?" I asked.

"Why, whatever makes you think I would be willing to hand him over to you two degenerates? You're a necromancer, Dancer, and you, Spark, well, I do like you my dear boy, but..."

"Okay," I sighed, "spill it. What do you want?"

"What makes you think I want anything?" he said, dropping the heart onto the scales, doing the lip-licking thing again.

"Because you always do."

"There is something you could do for me," he said cryptically.

"Okay." It wasn't going to be a request to be taken bowling.

You What!?

"No way. Out of the question. She's a sweet old lady and she doesn't do that kind of thing," I said, adamant.

"I'm not asking for you to arrange a night of debauchery with a selection of lubricants and rubberized paraphernalia," replied Stanley, looking hurt. I shuddered. "I'm asking if you'll put in a good word for me and arrange a date. Somewhere nice. I thought maybe Ginaro's. She likes Italian, doesn't she?"

"Well, yeah, she does. But goddammit, isn't there anything else you want?"

"Not really, no." Stanley smiled, and I shook like a spider was crawling toward my man bits, my hands tied behind my back, and I was being made to watch.

This was seriously bad news, I mean really bad.

Why would he ask if he knew it led nowhere? Was he asking because he knew he had to as it was his future, even if he got turned down? Or was he asking because he knew that somehow they did go on a date and then ended up living happily ever after?

He could become my step-granddad. It doesn't bear thinking about. Anything but that. Imagine, every time you saw him he'd know exactly what you were about to do or say, look at you with that all-seeing tilt of the head like he was bored yet amused at the same time.

"Fine. I'll ask Grandma if she will let you take her out on a date. But no funny business," I warned. "She's a sweet, innocent, gentle old lady and I won't have you taking advantage of my own flesh and blood."

"Heaven forbid, dear boy. I shall behave with the utmost respect. She is a fine specimen of womanhood, no doubt, and I will treat her as delicately as I treat my corpses." Stanley plopped a brain onto the scales. Respectfully, of course.

"That's what I'm worried about," I said under my breath.

"Pardon?"

"Nothing. Well, can we have the body?"

"It's over there." Stanley pointed to a drawer, so Dancer walked over and opened it. He's an old hand at this type of thing.

"Brr. Cold in here."

All three of us jumped, even Stanley. I looked at him suspiciously, but he just shrugged, and smiled, as if to say he'd done it the first time so he had to do it again. I don't know what's freakier, that, or vampires appearing from nowhere while you're in the morgue.

"What are you doing here?" I said.

Oliver smiled and replied, "Keeping an eye on you."

"I thought you'd gone." I wished he had.

"No, Spark. Not until you clean up your mess. I've been following you, making sure you do as you're told."

"Do as I'm told! You've got a bloody cheek, you lackey for—"

"Now, now, that's enough please, gentleman," interrupted Stanley. "Oliver, I would appreciate you coming into my place of work by normal means in the future, if you don't mind."

"I apologize," said Oliver. Even vampires are nice to Stanley, he creeps them out too.

"Accepted. Now, where were we?"

"I was about to take a look at the chess guy," said Dancer, ignoring Oliver. He hates him as much as I do—we bond over it and call him names behind his back. Well, to his face, usually.

"Let's get this done," I sighed.

I joined Dancer, and Stanley came too. So did Oliver, looking keen to witness the event he clearly knew was coming. He's annoying, but not stupid, so probably guessed what we had planned.

Stanley assumed a suitably inquisitive facial expression, as if not wanting to miss out on the action, and wondering how it would work. See, how could you live like that? He already knew what would happen, so why bother? I guess maybe some people enjoy their life so much they don't mind repeating it. I tried not to think of Grandma. Poor, innocent, sweet Grandma.

"Can you do it?" I asked Dancer.

He stared at me like I was an idiot. "Duh."

"Okay, I know you can do it. Can you do it so it seems genuine?"

"It will be genuine. I'm not an amateur you know. I take my work seriously."

"Don't we all," agreed Stanley.

"You're not a pathologist, Stanley. You're a mortuary technician and this is the morgue. Why are you always taking bits out of people?" Stanley went to answer, but I'd heard it all before. He doesn't trust the pathologists, and sometimes he just has a feeling about certain corpses. The annoying thing is he is always right —of course. "Okay, how long will it last, Dancer?"

"I can give you a few days at most, but that should be enough, right?"

"More than enough. I just need him up and about to stop all this from getting out of hand and to get me off the hook. You can do that?" I left it at that, but truth is I felt terrible and thought a few days of life was the least I could do. I felt bad for the medical staff involved, but if it avoided a vampire uprising, well, it was worth it.

"They'll still be looking for you though, won't they? For blasting him with your, you know?"

"Nobody sees us, do they? They won't find me. It's a precaution so nobody thinks the guy was killed by magic, that it was a mistake."

"Fine, whatever. You owe me though. Twice."

"Yeah, yeah, just do it."

"Okay, give me some room."

"Stanley, are you cool with this? Will you do some of that acting you are so famous for and pretend he was banging on the drawer and you let him out?"

"I'd love to, dear boy, but I'm afraid my shift ends in ten minutes and then it's over to Elaine."

"Ah, okay. That might work out better." Elaine is a Regular. No magic, just a technician, same as Stanley. If we could get the Grandmaster up and about before she turned up then it would be perfect.

"Okay, Dancer, do your ju-ju." He gave me the daggers—I knew that annoyed the hell out of him.

We moved away, but we all watched. You never tire of seeing somebody brought back from the dead— it's as close as we get to a true miracle, and fascinating in its morbidity.

As the cool air continued to escape from the drawer, Dancer removed the shroud from the man's body and draped it over the metal rail of the examination table.

Already I could feel the magic build and the sickness spread out like it was a black smoke drifting across the floor and creeping up my legs, entering my mouth, clawing into my lungs like glass and infecting my brain with its poison.

Sickness enveloped us all, and I watched through a fog of clawing demon limbs scratching at the surface of reality as the darkness became real. I tried to stay upright but ended up sat on the floor surrounded by the half-formed dream lives of trapped miscreants in the nether worlds.

I wasn't surprised to see Stanley beside me. Only difference was he looked like he was enjoying the show. Second time round I guess, makes all the difference.

Oliver joined us, more used to the dying than the actual dead. He wasn't coping any better than me, but still had that smackable sneer he wore like a mask of superiority that fooled nobody.

Dancer stood over the corpse, teeth clenched, face ashen, a blue vein throbbing at his temple like a worm trying to escape. He muttered whatever necromancers mutter to call forth the power to bring a person back from the dead.

You may think this is all going to result in some kind of zombie but the reality is different. This is proper magic, not anything half-arsed, certainly no magic-based virus. Dancer may be annoying and really slimy, but he knows his business. This was to be full-on resurrection. For a bit.

He waved his arms about, did well to fight back the souls trying to take advantage of the gaps in reality that such deep immersion in the Empty creates, and took in dark magic he could channel into the traces of what was once a living human being.

It was only four hours since the old guy had met his untimely demise, so he should be able to bring him back to full sentience, for a while, but these things aren't an exact science and there is no telling how it will work out until they sit upright, gasp, and begin to freak out.

Which is exactly what happened.

Dancer took a step back and silence descended. The demons disappeared, the sickness lifted—leaving its foul impression on reality behind—and I got up and pulled Stanley to his feet. I left Oliver where he was.

"Did it work?" I asked, peering at the still very dead looking Grandmaster.

"Yes, I think so. We just have to wait a minute."

"We better be quick, my shift ends in five and Elaine usually comes in early." Stanley hurriedly tidied away brains and assorted goop before it was time for him to leave.

"Just a second," said Dancer, staring at the corpse in anticipation.

The old guy sat bolt upright, gasped for air like a goldfish in a cracked aquarium, stared around with wild eyes all black from where I'd accidentally made them boil, just a bit—Dancer had done a fine repair job on them—then screamed at the top of his lungs. Not words, a primeval roar of absolute terror.

You couldn't blame him. After all, he'd just come back from the other side, whatever that meant for him personally.

Stanley pushed him down flat and slammed the drawer closed.

"Hey, you can't leave him like that, he'll freak," I said, feeling really bad for the old man.

"It will be for only a minute, and it's better than us all being discovered when Elaine arrives. You have to go, now." Stanley ushered us to the door, and we made to leave. He put an arm on my shoulder and said, "Don't forget your promise."

"I won't," I sighed. "I'll try, but there are no guarantees. And if she says yes then you better behave. Don't even think about preying on an old, innocent lady like Grandma. She's my only family."

Stanley held his hands up in protest. "I wouldn't dream of it, my dear boy. Or should I say, grandson?"

I felt like a thousand ice-cubes had been dropped down my underwear. Damn, was this him sharing what he knew to be the future? Or was he just going along with what he'd done in his life when he lived it for the first time and was making a rather tasteless joke?

You can see why seers like this are not easy to be around. It messes with your head something rotten.

We left, even Oliver, who looked worse than I felt.

The screaming from the drawer was really loud.

Is it Nice?

Out in the car park, we stood for a while sucking down deep lungfuls of fresh air, at least compared to the stink of the morgue. We watched Elaine as she rushed past us through the doors, seemingly late and looking flustered. Hopefully that would mean the poor guy wouldn't be screaming and freaked out for too much longer.

Stanley was right though, best she found him. It would make it a lot easier, and if he said that then it was the right thing to do. Maybe.

That's the real issue with seers—do they say things because it's the right thing and they know the results will be good, or do they stick exactly to the future they have already seen, be it good or bad? They never explain it properly so you never really know.

The drizzle resumed after a break to gather more depressing clouds, so we waited in the car. At least, me and Dancer did. Oliver hung around outside, didn't even ask to come in. He stood under the cover of the entry and observed the people coming and going.

"Will you look at that guy. Makes my skin crawl," said Dancer with a shudder.

"Says the man who just re-animated a corpse."

"That's different." He actually pouted. "Oliver there is looking for his next meal. He's preying on the weak, looking for someone too sad to care."

I watched Oliver for as long as I could stand, which was not long at all. Dancer was right, he was studying the people, stepping close to some, reading them, looking for pliable minds he could glamor now, eat later.

More than anything, I wanted to do something, but it's not my place, our place, and trying would lead to more death, more hurt, and it would never end.

In the end he got bored, and sat on the steps, waiting for me to leave. So he could follow, keep an eye on me until he felt satisfied.

I wanted to hang around and see what happened, and much as I would have liked to distance myself from the residue of magic clinging to the necromancer beside me, I knew it was best to have him close. Just in case. Raising the dead isn't always straightforward, so best to keep him nearby, for now.

"Where did he go?" I couldn't help it, I had to ask. I know the answer, but I also don't, if that makes sense? Death is funny like that—it's a bugger to believe in when you live the life our kind does.

Dancer sighed. We'd had the conversation before, or variations on it, and I'm sure that over the years he's had similar ones with no end of people and races. "Come on, Spark, seriously?"

"Hey, it's important. There is somewhere after, right? I mean, there has to be, otherwise how could you come back?"

"Of course there is somewhere after you die, what a stupid question." I didn't think it was stupid. It's the question we have striven to find an answer to ever since we could first think, and after billions upon billions of deaths there is still no proof that life after death exists. Not like, real proof.

There is faith, belief, all of that, but only people like Dancer know. Really know. I wanted to know too, although I already do I guess—death is far from the end of it all, it's just the beginning.

"Okay, what's it like then? When you go get them, bring them back?"

"It's different every time. The afterlife is what you want it to be. Not what you wish it was when you are alive, but what you feel is your due when you strip away all the ego and the wishful thinking. It's what you deserve."

Stuff of nightmares, isn't it? How do we know what we deserve? Some of the most evil people in history thought they were doing the right thing, so what does that say about the rest of us?

Dancer was serious for a moment and smiled knowingly as I got goosebumps.

"I know, right? Scary stuff. But it's private, Spark. I'm not about to tell of other people's afterlife, that's their business. But it's there, and, well, to be honest a lot of it isn't that nice. Sometimes it's so beautiful it hurts, in a nice way, but often..."

"So the answer is?"

"Be nice, cross your fingers, give up your seat for the elderly on the bus, recycle, try not to kill too many people, don't litter, a bit of praying never hurts, never, and I mean never, kick a dog, and hope for the best."

"Great," I said, feeling more depressed than ever.

"You asked."

We were both lost in our own thoughts. I can't imagine doing what Dancer does. Life is hard enough without having to go visit people in their own private purgatory or paradise after they think it's finally all over with—what a way to earn a living. Still, he seems to enjoy it. I guess everyone has a role to play in the game we call living and dying, and it's nice to know you have skills.

Half an hour later all hell broke loose.

Police cars, ambulances, hospital bigwigs—judging by the cars they drove and the suits they wore—and five minutes after that there were more TV crew vans than I'd seen that morning at the scene of the Grandmaster's murder. Now ex-murder.

Someone had spilled the beans. Hardly surprising, as it's a small city, so somebody would always be calling up their mum and gossiping, and she'd tell the next door neighbor and before you knew it people on the other side of the world knew that you'd broken up with your girlfriend. It's like social media, only without the annoying ads.

You can't beat the Welsh gossip grapevine for spreading news far and wide faster than a photon bouncing along a fiber optic cable.

I watched as one reporter, a man I recognized—he was from the BBC so this really had made it to the majors—stood on the steps and then spoke to the camera. Oliver even moved out of the way. I guess he thought it a bad idea to be filmed, especially considering the circumstances.

I couldn't hear a word though, so flipped open my phone and connected to their website.

"...an unexpected turn of events the Grandmaster reported murdered this morning has seemingly been discovered screaming and frantic in the morgue. Early reports indicate he seems nothing but distraught, with no signs of the fatalities reported earlier. This questions the whole validity of the mysterious events, suspected by some, haha, as being the first reported case of the true use of magic."

The reporter paused and put a hand to his ear. "I am getting reports... yes, there appears to be a number of new incidents popping up with various people witnessing more use of this black magic, people shooting what seems to be dark energy from their hands and causing physical harm to others. This seems to be happening worldwide and as of yet there are no known reasons why it should be suspected of being linked to what has happened here in Cardiff..."

I shut it down.

"Yes!"

"Seems to have worked then," said Dancer. He looked at me, eyebrows raised, still looking drained from his raising of the dead gig.

"Yeah. Um, thanks."

"You're welcome. Just remember—"

"Yeah, I owe you."

"Twice."

"I know."

Dancer smiled that creepy smile of his. "So, think this has done the trick then?"

"It'll help, and that other bit you heard on the news, the other reports, that's the final stage. In less than an hour it should all be done with."

"Why? What's going on?"

"Don't worry about it," I said as I started up the engine. "You'll find out soon enough. Right, I've got things to do. I've got to go to Kate's and then I guess I need to go see Grandma."

"Sounds good." Dancer beamed at me, or at least tried to. It came across more like he was constipated and really was trying his best to evacuate the problem.

"No chance."

"What? I like Grandma, although I'm not so sure she likes me that much. And I haven't seen Kate in a while. It'll be fun."

"Fun! I don't have time for fun. In case you haven't noticed, my life is on the line here. I have things to do. And I have to deal with the Armenian. You want to come along for that too?"

Dancer actually pulled away from me in the car, as if mentioning the woman could hurt him. So much for the terrifying necromancer image.

"She's behind what you did? Christ, you are screwed. Why bother with this then, trying to fix it, bringing the old guy back, if you are done for anyway?"

"Hey!" I protested. "Have some faith. Rikka sent me to deal with her yesterday apparently, so that means I must have thought I could handle Ankine Luisi, so—" We both shuddered at the name.

"But you didn't, did you? You got stitched up good and proper and you're gonna go back for more."

"It's not like I have a choice, is it? Rikka said sort this then deal with Ankine Luisi, and when Rikka says do something—"

"You do it. Well, good luck." Dancer opened the car door and was gone.

So much for loyalty amongst the dark magic wielders.

At least I didn't have to deal with his stink of death. Dancer reeks of morgues, cemeteries, and hospitals. He's been around them so long it's like the smells of decay, strong bleach, and formaldehyde seep from his skin and come out of his lungs when he exhales.

I settled back and closed my eyes for a moment, enjoying the new car smell.

What a morning. I wished it was over, but my day was only just beginning.

The Unviral Viral Vampire Caper

"Hey," I said as Kate unlocked then opened the door to my timid knocking.

"Hey," she said, smiling, just a hint of canine. She was less aware she was doing it than she used to be, the vampire nature slowly taking over, but damn, it was still a beautiful smile.

Like a ray of sunshine as you ran toward the precipice of your future, not caring if you fell into oblivion as long as you could take the smile with you to comfort you through your lonely eternity.

Well, so far so good. I was feeling rather nervous after the way we'd said goodbye earlier. I didn't know what to expect and my heart was fluttering like a schoolboy's with a crush—okay, it always does that around Kate, but this was different as I wasn't sure what the deal was.

I followed Kate back into her kitchen and a quick look at her face told me everything was fine. It would work its way out one way or the other, the main thing was we would remain friends. That was all that counted—yeah, I'm a liar, even to myself. I wanted to rip her clothes off, lick her perfectly curved bottom and... She put the kettle on; I needed a cold shower.

"All done. Wanna see?"

"Sure, please. I can't thank you enough for this, Kate. I don't know what I'd do without you. Hey, I have to go to Grandma's next, you wanna come say hi? You know how much she likes seeing you."

"That would be great." Kate opened up the laptop while the kettle boiled and clacked away like the pro she is.

I stared at her profile as the sun made a quick breakthrough before being beaten back down by the angry clouds. Something wasn't quite right. She looked old, normally smooth skin mottled and wrinkled a little, eyes heavy and that abundance of life not there.

Kate isn't exactly beautiful, not in a classical way. She is just... Gosh, how do you describe someone that is more beautiful than a butterfly or a faery, or a sunset, even though to others they may see nothing but a somewhat attractive lady? Kate is intoxicating, and it isn't the vampire that makes her that way—although I guess it does add something. It's her. It's Kate. The whole package. She's a nice person in a sea of slime.

Her nose is a little too large, her blue eyes are too big, which is ace, her lips are awesome, full and pouting, and her blond hair slides about when she moves her head. And she laughs a lot, which is like a smack across the head with a bag of faery dust, so, yeah, I guess she is beautiful. To me.

But she wasn't herself, and I'd been self-centered asking her to do work for me when I should have seen the signs earlier.

"Ready?" she asked, about to show me her handy work.

"In a minute. How long since you fed?"

Kate looked me in the eye and said, "A few months, maybe longer." She wouldn't try to hide it from me; we were past such things. We both knew the score, both knew what she was and what her new life entailed, and she said it without remorse, without apology. She answered with thanks. Thanks for asking, thanks for noticing, and thanks for helping with what she knew I would help with.

I nodded, and the agreement was made. Nothing more was needed.

We got back to the business at hand, and I ignored her shaking hands—you think going cold turkey with the booze is tough? You know nothing.

In both her previous life, and her new one, Kate worked freelance as one of those miracle-makers with video. She's not exactly a special effects person, neither is she a game designer, but rather, she works with fringe outfits making short snippets for promotions. Be it bands, bloggers, or the latest guru of this or that craze, and when she gets low on jobs—which is seldom —or wants to get creative, she can put together a short sequence that is almost guaranteed to gain a little notoriety and earn her revenue as it gets shared around the Web and picks up money from clicks on ads served alongside her creation.

She had excelled herself for me.

As I watched, mesmerized by her skill, the power of modern technology, and the ability for online content to spread around the globe faster than the Welsh gossip grapevine, I knew I was saved.

Kate had manipulated a number of recorded deaths that had occurred that very day around the world, of which there were countless. It was a mean thing to do, messing with people's last breath like that, but it saved the world, and that was more important.

She had added everything from lightning bolts coming from the fingers or eyes of people stood watching as terrible accidents happened, to dark and menacing black clouds of death full of spectral ghosts appearing from out of people's mouths and attacking unfortunate souls who keeled over and died.

On and on it went, over twenty of them in total, spreading around the globe at the speed of light and making my indiscretion of the morning insignificant and lost amid a sea of nonsense. The number of views was staggering, let alone the comments of the crazies that believed or disbelieved what they were seeing. Most knew the score in the age where anything could be manipulated, but it didn't stop them being shared on every possible social media platform and the regular news.

The finale was one she had just created and sent less than ten minutes ago, showing world leaders from the US, the UK, Russia, and Korea all performing one kind of magical act or another in quick succession and looking entirely believable, followed by a mash-up of all the clips she had created playing fast but in reverse, recordings of her work environment showing exactly how it was done.

"You are a lifesaver." I went to kiss her, then thought better of it and instead half punched her arm—don't you dare laugh.

She looked at me like I was a complete idiot then smiled, shook her head in exasperation and giggled.

"I like you too."

"Of course, why wouldn't you? Dark Magic Enforcer, Faz Pound has a way with the ladies."

Kate thumped right back, only hard.

Vampires have some serious power behind them, and she knocked me right off my stool and halfway across the room. I slammed into the spotless wooden floor like I'd been hit by a wrecking ball.

"See, smooth." I groaned as Kate jumped down off her stool and was at my side faster than you can say, "Vampires are really fast," concern on her face.

"Oh my god, I'm so sorry, Faz." She burst out crying.

I held her there on the floor for a while. It wasn't the first time. Her life took a lot of getting used to, and when the tears dried up we got up and left, coffee forgotten, the work she'd done to cover up my accidental revelation of magic put out of our minds, only one thing now the focus.

Kate needed to feed, so we had to go find someone she could kill and still find a way to carry on living with ourselves afterward.

Such is the life of a vampire and the friend of a vampire. But I'm Faz Pound, Dark Magic Enforcer, Puncher on the Arm of Hot Vampires, Slayer of Erotic Moments, Destroyer of Intimacy, Ignorer of all the Signs, the Dolt who Rules all Dolts, and all round muppet, but what I am not is someone who abandons friends or turns from helping them kill someone to drink their blood.

Why?

Because Kate and I made a pact the first day she awoke in Grandma's house after I saved her and she understood who she was—she only kills people that deserve to die. It's a win-win situation.

Hunting Bad Guys

We have a list. Actually, I have a list I let Kate peek at as and when needed. No point putting temptation in her way, and besides, she's intelligent enough to know it's best not to have so many addresses to hand. It's much better to have the information when it's needed—it makes us both sleep better at night, or usually day in her case.

Nobody wants to know what their next meal is all the time—you need the element of surprise—so she's no different in that regard than the rest of us.

"I'm sorry about this, Faz."

"About what? Hey, I'm here for you, always. You just saved my bacon, and don't tell anyone, but I was getting seriously worried for a while there. Anyway, I'd do anything for you, you know that."

"But it's so gross! How can you stand it?" Kate isn't a fan of the gore and the screaming side of her new life, but what can you do?

"Trust me, I've seen worse. A lot worse. You should have seen it back in the early nineteen hundreds. People were really dramatic then, and we had no TV or Internet so everyone took things a lot more seriously. At least now people half believe in magic and vampires and the Empty anyway. It makes life easier."

"Also a lot riskier. Do you think the videos will get you off the hook? I hope so."

"Definitely. You saved me. My messed up morning will be forgotten now, no doubt about it. You even reverse engineered the footage of it so it looks like you made that one up too, so I'm fine. Oh, and I had Dancer bring back our favorite chess player for a few days so I'm absolutely in the clear. Sort of a backup plan just to keep everyone happy. A distraction, and I owed the poor guy a few more days, to say sorry."

"By everyone you mean Taavi and Rikka, right?"

"Yeah, exactly. I'll have to pop in and see him later, tell our esteemed leader I've been a good boy. Amongst other things."

"Like what?"

"Don't you worry about it. We'll do this, go see Grandma, then you can sleep and recover. You okay?" I took a quick glance and she seemed all right. A little more tired but nothing too drastic. Much better than she had near the beginning when she fought the urge and paid the consequences. If she was up for letting me help then I knew she needed it, as letting the hunger build for too long is probably worse than anything I've had to deal with in the course of enforcing and letting the Empty consume me.

"Fine. Just a little sleepy, and hungry."

"We'll be there soon. Get some rest."

Kate slept while I drove out of the city and headed toward our destination. I couldn't help wondering where Oliver was, and if he'd given up on shadowing me. Maybe he had, but something told me he'd be back soon enough. Probably off feeding on one of the unfortunates he'd picked at the hospital. I put him out of my mind. I never dwell on things out of my control, what's the point?

My spirits were high as I knew I would be in the clear. Disaster averted, at least for now, although I knew I had the worst to come: Ankine Luisi. But before I tackled that terrifying problem I'd go see Rikka again and get more information on what exactly may have happened the night before and why I'd been sent in the first place.

The night was still a blur. I remembered nothing of my encounter with her, just what the outcome was, and the last thing I wanted was a repeat of that—one dead chess player, or dead, now re-animated, soon to be dead again anyway.

What a life. It beats wearing a tie and sitting in a cubicle though.

Sometimes.

*

"We're here. Kate, time to wake up." She stirred slowly, like she could hardly hear or function, buried deep in sleep and a weariness only the vampire can know. I knew it would be a minute or so before she came around properly. The changes in just three years were subtle, but they were there. Once she would have snapped to attention, now it was like waking a baby after a bottle of milk.

I wound the window down and new car smell was replaced with the beautiful aroma of clean air. Grass and cows and rain. Not city rain, proper, fresh, uncontaminated rain that washes away your sins and allows you to believe, just for a while, that the world is a simple place and it all makes sense.

Droplets splashed onto my face through the open window as I let my mind clear and soak up the purity of a world devoid of intentions good or bad. A world where everything just was, how it has always been for the planet. It's only people and other sentient species that have existential angst and try to do the other person over to get ahead in life.

Something caught my eye and the purity left, replaced by anger and even a little hate, although I don't have a lot of hate left in me. I've seen too many truly bad things—as much from Regulars as from Hidden—to have more than a tiny hard lump buried somewhere I can't find left of that emotion. It's a battle, this life, and some people are just plain wrong. Aberrations that make the world a little worse to live in.

We were about to make it a tiny bit safer, for a while.

Kate woke and smiled at me, making everything better.

"He's over there, in the field. Looks like he's shifting stuff with his tractor. You want me to come with you?"

"No, but thanks. I'll be fine. Tell me what he did again, Faz, just so I know I'm not a terrible person."

I leaned over and cupped her face in my hands. "Hey, you are a good person. You make the world shine. You don't kill just to survive. You made a choice, to only do it to the bad, and that makes you good."

"But there are laws. Who are we to judge? Who am I?"

"Come on, we've had this conversation before. I'm not going to try to convince you, Kate, this is your decision. You know who you are, what he is. It's up to you." It is. This is her life. I'm not about to goad her into murder. To take a life is a terrible thing, but sometimes the laws of man fail, so sometimes the only justice that remains is carried out outside of the law of the land. It is no less righteous, it just doesn't come with paperwork.

"Sorry, I'm being silly. See you soon?"

"Sure. Be safe."

Kate got out and closed the door gently behind her. I watched as she wrapped her coat around herself tightly, then trudged across the field toward the slow moving tractor and the man driving it.

I got out of the car and fumbled around on the back seat, opened up the bag I'd grabbed from Kate's, as she never remembered, and got things ready.

Am I a bad man for doing this? Who decides? I'll tell you what a bad man is, then maybe I will leave it to you. I am at peace with who I am, most of the time, but it still leaves a nasty taste in my mouth, the death. Even when the death is of a Mr. Ronald Dickinson; farmer, loner, and murderer of young children.

Ronald is on the list, but there are names above his, and they are all crossed out. It's grim, it's nasty, it's the life I know, and many would thank me and Kate for what we do. Others would lock us up, Kate especially, as she does the killing, and throw away the key.

I'm confident we are doing the right thing, usually.

This man, this farmer, killed two children one night in a rage of epic proportions and it had nothing to do with being drunk, being off his meds, or anything else that could go a little way to downgrading his actions from despicable to excusable in even a minor degree by way of diminished responsibility.

He is, was, bad to the core. Something could be done about him. Yes, there are countless vampires just as nasty, but even they self-police, and although not averse to killing anyone they please, they draw the line at children—you do not want to know what they do to their kind that take the life of what they hold in the highest regard, and see as the only pure thing on the planet. Innocent children are untouchable, even to the oldest, nastiest vampires still alive.

I won't go into the details of what this "man" did, but our world is a small world and we hear things. We hear, and know, more than you can imagine. When Regulars slip through the cracks of what is right and decent, yes, even to us, then don't be surprised if they get what is due somewhere down the line.

I have contacts. I know people, and they know people, and some of us are even living lives in normal professions in the Regular world and like that kind of life. But some things nobody can stomach, be they on one side of the law or the other, and that is the harming, or worse, of animals and children. The vampires regard them as the only pure things on the planet.

He got what he deserved, but nobody will ever know what happened, and the only people that will remember his name are me, Kate, and the parents of the children they will never get to see grow up.

Kate came back to the car ten minutes later, looking vibrant but with the weight of the world on her shoulders at the same time. She was still feeling the sickness after feeding, that was clear, but it would pass soon enough. The blood magic that coursed through her veins, and would keep her strong and in superhuman condition for months on end, battled the sickness. It was clear which was winning.

She had a vitality to her now that was unmistakable to the likes of me. Kate practically glowed with inner happiness and contentment, and I could see the guilt and shame wash away as the effects of the blood took over.

This is the true horror of what she is, and what I know she will become as the years pass. She had her fix and she was happy, for now, and the blood magic wrapped her in its cold and numbing embrace.

Escape was impossible now. She was vampire and always would be, and the guilt over what she did would lessen each time she took a life, until it meant nothing at all and then she would be lost. Her humanity stripped away and her attitude to human beings nothing more than ours toward the meat we consume without a thought for the animal it came from.

Depressing stuff, but she looked hot, even covered in blood and gristly bits.

"Here, I got your change of clothes ready. Have some wipes." I couldn't take my eyes off her as she cleaned her face free of another human being while looking in the side mirror, fangs stained red, lips too full, eyes dancing with merriment and vigor, her entire body somehow screaming more sexiness than was decent. Then she stripped off her coat and blouse. I nearly fainted.

The draw of a freshly fed vampire is too much for the human mind and loins to stand, and it doesn't matter if it's a man or a woman, young or old. It's the magic, the blood magic that draws you in and awakens your own body in ways impossible to describe.

I can't imagine what sex must be like at a moment like that, and I was having a hard time stopping myself jumping on her right there and then as her breasts seemed to have grown a few sizes and pushed at her bra like... You get the idea.

She was feeling it too, I knew, but it wasn't what I wanted although I wanted it more than anything. So I turned away, handed her a clean blouse, and rummaged round in the bag for her even though there was nothing else to get.

"Sorry," said Kate as she appeared beside me, dressed and clean.

"Don't be."

"I just wish..."

"So do I, Kate, so do I. Let's go visit Grandma, have a cup of tea."

"Thanks, Faz. I mean it."

"I know you do. I know."

We drove off in silence. Someone would be along to clean up the mess. It's a vampire thing, they have "people" for it, some kind of vampire communication so they always know when someone has fed. Vampires are never alone, they all belong to a House, and Kate belongs to House Taavi, who also happens to be Head of the UK Vampire Council.

Why? Because I'd killed her maker and he belonged to House Taavi, that's why. The maker had been under Taavi's control so he inherited her, and you don't get to have a say in such things.

She is his. Forever.

A Visit to Grandma's

"Grandma? Are you home?"

"What have you done to your hair!? Change it back, right this minute." Grandma stood in the hallway, wearing her perpetually clean pinafore, her pink house slippers—although I've never heard of "outside the house" slippers—with her hands on her hips. She inspected me like she would a selection of dubious meat at a butcher's closing down sale then wagged her finger at me.

"You look like a pop star." She didn't mean it in a good way.

I can never win with Grandma. When I let my hair grow she said I looked like a hippie and told me to get it cut. Now that I had she wanted it back to being long, and dark, even though I distinctly remember years ago her telling me I should dye it light as I looked too depressing and like a funeral director. That's Grandma for you, and I love her more than life itself.

"Aw, Grandma, why—" My only living flesh and blood held up a hand and stopped me mid-sentence. She'd said her piece, now it was done— Grandma doesn't dwell on the past, she is a forward thinker, a positive and strong woman.

Kate smirked beside me.

"Ooh, hello dear. How are you? Are you two an item yet, eh?" Grandma wiggled her eyebrows, then her ears. I swear she would have gone, "Nudge, nudge, wink, wink," if I hadn't interrupted. Kate was loving every minute of it. The pair of them had hit it off the instant they met.

"I can't change it back. I cut it." I complained like a grumpy teenager.

"Hi, Grandma Pound, you look well," said Kate, playing the perfect future granddaughter-in-law. I wish!

"Don't be daft," scolded Grandma, giving me a final dressing down with a glance before dismissing me. "And you look as pretty as always, Kate." She turned and walked back to the kitchen at the rear of the house, calling over her shoulder, "If you can grow back heads you can grow back hair."

"Heads? Who can grow back heads? If you lose your head you won't have a brain so how could you grow it back? And I know I can grow back hair, but I'm not going to force it. It does it on its own."

"Does it? Does it really?" Grandma said cryptically.

"Um, I think so." Grandma can do that to you. She confuses you, gets you in a muddle, and you walk away not sure if you have to use a little magic to make your hair and fingernails grow or if it just, you know, happens. It does, right? See what I mean?

"She's so sweet," said Kate, smiling at me like I'd brought her to pick a puppy.

"You always say that." I put a hand through my hair and tried to think about how keratin synthesis worked.

"Because she is." Kate left me to my musings and followed Grandma into the kitchen.

I can't tell you how pleased I am that the two favorite women in my life hit it off so well. When I brought Kate to Grandma's that very first time, Kate was in a terrible way, almost dead.

Her maker had been a bad character, and the last thing on his mind had been another vampire to add to his Ward. So Kate was either lucky or unlucky that we brought her back from the brink, depending on your outlook on such things.

I'd found her, dealt with the maker as I'd been sent to do, and rushed Kate to Grandma's as I lost the plot a little and didn't know what else to do.

As Kate recovered, the two women bonded in a way I know I will never understand, and I'm sure that whatever happens with me and Kate—if we stay friends, or more, or not—Kate and Grandma will always be part of each other's lives.

Kate has no family, so maybe that explains the relationship, or maybe it's just because they like each other and see a little of themselves in the other woman. Don't ask me, I'm a man and apparently we aren't built to understand these types of relationships, or so they keep telling me at any rate. I don't argue—I'd lose.

My promise to Stanley tapped at my mind like a goblin playing ping pong against the wall of my skull with a blowfish, so I took a deep breath and stepped into the lion's den, otherwise known as the kitchen.

The two women were deep in conversation over by the stove, and I wondered for the millionth time how Grandma could stand the heat and the smell. The room was like the devil's sauna and the smell was worse than the time I had to dig up the body of Franco the Toe Eater and he fell apart in my hands.

An ancient extractor fan clattered and sucked, but it was no match for what it faced. It did what it could but it never seems to make any difference. Grandma never notices anyway.

Hoping there would be tea—Grandma makes the best tea in the world—I removed my jacket and hung it over the back of a chair older than most vampires. The rest of the furniture in the house is the same. Not exactly antique in the "This is old and expensive" way, just old and familiar. Like the baby blanket you still clutch at night now and then when you are feeling extra sad and alone. Yeah, I know, that's just me again, isn't it?

"Have you fixed it?" asked Grandma, turning from her bubbling pots and smiling the smile of a woman that knows all and there is no place to hide.

"I think so. Kate saved me with some seriously cool editing, and, er, Dancer helped me with a slight issue at the morgue. He says hi, by the way." Don't ask how she knew, she always does.

"You were a very silly boy, Faz. What were you thinking? That poor man. You shouldn't take games so seriously."

"Me! He was the one that went off on one. But anyway, it was an accident. I didn't know what I was doing."

"Of course. You wouldn't have done such a silly thing otherwise. But Kate stopped you getting into any more trouble, didn't you, Kate?" Grandma gave her a kiss and Kate beamed at me, loving being given all the credit.

"Hey, I've been busy as hell, um, very busy this morning, and it isn't over yet."

"You be careful with her. The Armenian is trouble."

"How do you know about..." There was no point in asking. Grandma always knows. "I'll be careful. Tea?"

"Coming right up. It's brewing. I put it on five minutes before you came, so it will be nice and strong now."

Again, no point asking how she knew we were coming. It would be like interrogating a bird to find out how it knew how to fly.

Kate joined me at the table after putting coasters out for each of us. Grandma graciously opened the large window above the sink that overlooks a garden that always brings a smile to my face no matter my mood.

The cool, sweetly scented air invaded the kitchen like it had an important job to do, which it did, and soon the cloying atmosphere was replaced with the freshness of semi-rural suburban Cardiff and the aromas of untold herbs and all manner of exotic medicinal plants. Not to mention a few that, if mixed in the right combination, could do anything from turn you into a frog to make you irresistible to the opposite, or same, sex.

Grandma had explained her potions to me long ago, and often over the years, so it was pretty much second nature now when it came to understanding exactly what she did, and it isn't what you think.

As I sucked in the sweet smell of a thousand plant species, I thought about how the human mind works and the connection between us and the Empty. It's more bizarre than you could imagine.

People like Grandma, I guess you'd call them witches—although that means about as much as calling me a wizard—understand the human mind like nobody else can. She's more a psychologist than anything else, able to peel back the layers of protection human beings and other species hide behind and get to the truth of the problem.

When people come to see Grandma for her services—and you would not believe how much she charges without batting a wrinkly eyelid—she doesn't sit them in a chair, ask them what potion they want and then cook it up and it's job done. It goes further than that, much further, and the potion is the last piece of a complex jigsaw puzzle.

My Grandma, perfect, lovely, kind-hearted and adorable old lady that she is, brings her clients to tears, to rage, to ranting and raving, to breaking down and spilling their deepest and darkest secrets with her gentle words, and her insistence on getting to the truth of the matter. Her clients pay her handsomely for the privilege.

She listens, she asks the right questions, and what none of them realize—Regulars, or Hidden—is that she is manipulating their body chemistry through her words and priming them for what is to come. It's a subtle art, and nearly every witch you could ever hope to meet is a charlatan. But not Grandma.

Hormones are adjusted, mental states are aroused, and emotions are directed with her subtle, and not-so-subtle, manipulations. States of being are altered and neural pathways are opened, or closed on a door to a room full of the baggage of a lifetime since it isn't important at that moment. And over the course of sometimes a few minutes, sometimes a few hours, sometimes days or weeks, she puts you into a place where she knows you are as receptive to her own version of the Empty and her potions as you could possible be.

It's a mental game, and so complex I still have no clue how it works, but it's all to do with the power of emotion and the control it can have over our own minds and bodies.

When her clients finally drink the potion prepared for them, the myriad ingredients she has chosen carefully, and mixed in the exact right way, act like an explosive awakening and anything, and I mean anything, is then possible.

Something is awoken inside. Your mind, already primed, is extremely receptive to the liquid gold that slides down your throat sending signals that alter you either forever or for a fleeting moment, depending on what you have asked for, but usually what she decides is best for you whether you know it or not.

People leave not feeling like they could rule the world, but with the ability to do so. Suicidal teenagers leave understanding that death comes to us all and is never to be hurried. They are given not only the knowledge of what lies beyond, and the realization that they can overcome any obstacle, but the actual proof. This is not just belief, but something as real as Grandma's power itself.

Poor people leave with a blueprint for success that many never implement as they also know that money seldom equals happiness. And rich people depart knowing their money is genuinely what makes them happy, and they no longer spend sleepless nights worrying about the unjust distribution of wealth.

She never gives people what they think they want, she gives them what they need—her counsel and her potions unlock the reality of what it is to be a human being or one of the true Hidden—and reconfigures the self into what it has always wanted to be deep down, even if you didn't know it or even imagined it was who you really were.

But above all, she makes the best cup of tea in the world.

This is what it means to be a witch, what it really means. It's about understanding people, being kind and considerate, and a hard-headed woman who knows best and will never take no for an answer.

Grandma has also been known to kill clients within moments of meeting them. Like I said, she knows what's best for you, and for the world.

So if you ever pay her a visit, be damn sure you deserve this life you've been granted before you accept a cup of tea and sip it while she smiles at you with that twinkle in her eye, then calls Rikka for a Cleaner as she picks up the pieces of the shattered china, and puts a tea towel over your head so she doesn't have to look at your contorted face as rigor mortis sets in.

Man, I love this woman. She's the nicest lady you could ever hope to meet.

Did I mention she is almost as old as Taavi, the vampire? No? Well, she is, and one of her looks is a lot scarier than anything you could imagine him doing to you.

I love her more than anything, and she truly is the kindest and sweetest person I have ever met. There is no falseness; she is an elemental force of nature. You could no more call her impure than you could a lion cruel for hunting to feed itself, or to accuse the wind of being mean for rippling through the grass gently on a perfect summer's day.

She just is. Like nature, only without the volcanoes and the disease and the mass destruction.

This is why some call real witches Mother—it's a long tradition and goes back to when they were called Mother Nature's Helpers. And it's apt.

She is her.

Perfect.

Grandma.

Thick liquid poured from the teapot into three cups and I swallowed nervously.

"Um, Grandma, you like Italian, right?"

Her eyes lit up and she licked her lips. "Ooh, yes. You know me and meatballs, it's my favorite."

Here went nothing.

Seriously?

"What do you mean you'd love to go out with Stanley?" Kate nudged me in the ribs. "Ow! What?"

"Grandma said yes. I think it's sweet," Kate said, smiling.

"Sweet! He's a seer and he's seen the future. His whole life! Which means he knows what happens to all of us if we are a part of it."

"Well, I think he's a real gentleman," said Grandma, poking at her hair like she was going on the date in a few minutes.

"He works in the morgue," I protested. "He knows his future and he drops brains into trays for a living. Not even for a living. He does it because he enjoys it! Did I mention he knows his entire life already?"

"And he is always very polite and smiles a lot. Plus, I haven't been out with a man for..." Grandma counted on her fingers. "Gosh, a very long time.

Probably almost a century. Whoo, time flies when you're busy, busy, busy."

I can't actually remember Grandma ever going on a date, or anything like that. To be honest, until then I never saw her as a sexual person—she's Grandma! Was I being overly protective? Maybe. But it was Stanley. Stanley! He would know exactly how the date would go, would know what happened in the future, and he may even know my future. It gives me the creeps, okay?

"He's always made me feel safe when our paths have crossed. Like he's looking out for you and knows what's best. He has such a nice manner about him." Grandma looked like she was reminiscing about past men she'd known.

Had she known any? I guess she must have. After all, I was here, wasn't I? She is my mother's mother, so I know she must have had a relationship. Heck, she was married to my grandfather, a Regular, but that was long before I was ever around.

To me, she is this lovely old lady that makes tea and helps solve other people's problems, so it felt odd to be having the conversation, and Kate wasn't helping.

"I can do your hair and makeup if you like," offered Kate.

"Ooh, that would be lovely. When does he want to take me? Did he say?"

"Um, no, he just wanted me to ask if you would like to go out with him. You're serious, right? You want to?"

"Of course. I am a woman, you know, not just your grandmother."

I said nothing as she was right, but I never thought of her like that. She's more like a natural element than someone who likes to go out on dates with friendly mortuary technicians that can see the future.

The uncomfortable silence grew, the only sounds the bubbling of the pots and the birds singing happily in the garden. They looked after Grandma's plants, clearing away the bugs, just the bad bugs mind you—apparently she has an agreement with the sparrows. No, I have never asked what it is. Some things are witch concerns only.

I sipped my tea, wondering how things were going with the chess player, and the media misdirection Kate had instigated, then thought maybe I should have a shower.

"You should have a shower," said Grandma. "You stink worse than a dung sprite. Did you know that I once met one when I was on holiday in Scotland and it..."

Kate and Grandma got into a long conversation about the merits of dung sprites, and I sniffed my armpits, recoiled in horror, then tried to plan out the rest of my day. Kinda pointless—being an enforcer means that life is always full of surprises along with periods of utter boredom—but I really did need a shower.

Exhaustion took over and I sank low in my chair while I let the voices lull me into a state that has saved my life and my sanity on numerous occasions.

I let my tattoos pulse gently, like a physical, warm caress I hadn't had for so long, and felt the connection between myself and the Empty. The sickness threatened me, like I would roll over into fetid water and be sucked down into mud that would keep me there for lifetimes, but it passed as I surrendered. Almost without thought, I tweaked the energy and let its power invade me, give me what I needed.

This is a gift for wizards. It's why we can keep going so long, why we often stink a little, and why we often have terrible dark bags under our eyes. You can beat nature for a while, but as with all things, there are consequences.

A few minutes later I snapped out of it, feeling like I'd slept all night. There was this familiar buzz going that I let slide back down the fuzzy pathways of my mind, or I'd be manic and Grandma would accuse me of doing drugs again.

What remained was a clarity, an alertness, and a sense of needing to get things done. Plus the stink, that was still there. Magic can do many things, but act as soap, deodorant, and aftershave it cannot.

"...gave me a mushroom in the shape of a willy and I stuck it..." I zoned back out quickly. I really didn't want to hear the end of that particular story of Grandma's.

Lalalalala occupied my mind while I fought with the words trying to stake into my ears like pencils fresh from the sharpener, tipped with sexual innuendo from a two thousand year old family member. I jumped like a frog carried into the kitchen by Grandma as I felt a tap on my shoulder.

"There's someone here to see you." Grandma looked less than pleased.

"Here?" I looked around the room but it was just me, Grandma, and Kate.

"Down here."

I looked down at the deep baritone of a familiar voice. "Oh, hi, Intus. What's up?"

Intus scowled and bunched tiny fists. Word of caution. Think before you talk to imps. They get touchy if they think you're trying to make fun of their size. Intus seemed to mull over my words, decided I could live a few more minutes, and relaxed.

"Sorry for the intrusion, Mrs. Grandma,"—imps are very formal—"but this couldn't wait."

"That's all right, Intus. Would you like a cup of tea?"

"Oh, no, thank you. I drank not long ago, must have only been a few years. I don't want to get bloated. Got to look after the body and all that, especially now. But thank you for your kind offer."

"No problem. Well, I'll leave you and Kate to it then. I have things to do. Faz, you be out of here soon. I have a client. You be careful." Grandma scowled at my hair then continued lecturing. "All this dashing about, playing with Inter Webs and dragging poor Kate into this. Tut-tut. And do something about that hair!"

"Yes, Grandma. Sorry, Grandma. Thanks for the tea. We'll be off now." I gave her a kiss and Kate did likewise. Intus bellowed farewell and we headed out into the front garden.

You know what? The one thing I will forever love my Grandma for, and I know it's why Kate loves her like her own flesh and blood, is that she never once gave even the slightest hint of disapproval as to Kate's "condition." There has never been any judging, no slurs on the type of creature she now is, or what she will most likely become over the decades if she survives.

Grandma has always treated Kate as an equal, and Grandma hates vampires with a vengeance that knows no bounds.

After all, they killed her husband, killed my mother and father. She may be a loving, caring woman, but one thing she never does is forgive.

Out in the garden, as we walked down the drive, Intus morphed from a five centimeter imp into a rather odd looking cat. Imps aren't the best at shifting, it's not a part of who they are, but it beats talking to a bright red mini person at any rate.

Intus is an imp enforcer, dealing strictly with the imp side of things, and trust me, it keeps my friend very busy. Imps are, and I'm trying to be diplomatic, rather excitable at times, and like nothing better than when things get chaotic.

They also like to amuse themselves by going into people's houses and moving stuff about, knocking things over, getting together and hiding under sheets or biting your ear and making you scream and generally freak out—in other words, enforcing punishment and dealing with the spillover of magic into normal life is a full-time job for Intus, and then some.

Poor thing is always run ragged, but Intus is a happy imp. It's not their nature to be morose.

Which is why I knew this was serious. Intus hadn't even cracked a joke yet.

An Imp Interlude

Imps are nice. I like them. They are often funny, sometimes annoying—as they don't know when enough is enough—and have this rather crazed need to play jokes and generally get into mischief. But they don't mean anything by it, they are just expressing their nature.

They're a kind of devil, or a demon, I guess, but a special kind. Nice.

They are immortal—you just try to kill one, it's impossible—and I've always wondered how old that makes them as they still have to be born, right? Plus, there are baby imps, although I've only ever seen one, and they are more prevalent than you would think.

They are usually bright red, sometimes mottled with brown, have big ears (for their size), long forked tails, and clawed hands that can do serious damage even to humans, or any other species for that matter. They are also incredibly strong. And I have absolutely no idea how you tell if they are female or male, much like dwarves in that regard.

I once asked Intus if it were a male or female and it went off on this mad tirade about not being put in a gender-confined box, and wasn't this the modern age where everyone was judged not on their sexuality but the kind of person they were? And how would I feel if it went around asking me if I was a man or a woman? To which I replied, I didn't mind, and I was a man. Which confused the hell out of my friend, and it asked me how did you tell? I tried to explain, but it didn't compute, so there are always two sides to every story you see.

All I know is that imps are like crazed children after being let loose in a sweet shop for an hour and then force-fed high sugar content drinks and then told to go have fun and see how much trouble they can cause—meaning enforcers are kept on their claws.

From what I can gather, there is an enforcer imp for every ten or so of their kind, and even that is hardly enough. They don't seem to sleep often, and when they do it's for weeks, months, sometimes years at a time. They consume pure magic for sustenance, although will eat or drink now and then just for the novelty factor. And they deal with their own business.

For Intus—all imp names begin with I—to come and ask for help concerning imp related matters meant things were not good, and it wasn't like I had a free afternoon to just help out. But this particular imp is a friend, so I couldn't say no.

One thing I knew above all else was that I was starving hungry. I should have asked Grandma for something, but let's just say she has a habit of slipping a few herbs in with your sandwich, and I really couldn't face any alterations to my already unstable mind and body.

What a morning! It's not always like this. Usually I laze about and drink coffee, but such is the life of a wizard enforcer—always something to surprise you.

"Let's get into the car. You can turn back from that... It is a cat, right?" I asked Intus.

"Of course I'm a cat. What else would I be?"

"Maybe a crushed miniature tiger," offered Kate.

Intus scowled at us both, then laughed that deep laugh of its. There's no keeping it down. Oops, I mean depressed.

I opened up the car and they both jumped in. Intus stood on the dashboard and scowled at the hanging pine-tree-shaped air freshener—they have sensitive noses. Long too.

"Okay, what's up, Intus? But I have a busy day so please make it quick."

"I heard. Sounds like you are dealing with it though." Imps know pretty much everything that goes on. It's what makes them so useful, so dangerous too. "I don't know why you don't just, you know, come out. It would make it easier."

"What, like your kind have?"

"Hey, it's not in our nature to tell the world about us. Where's the fun in that? We wouldn't be able to move things around in human's fridges if they knew it was us. And who's going to steal all the single socks and put keys in different pockets and put cash back in your trousers even though you were sure you took it out before you put them in the washing machine? These things don't get done by themselves, you know. And what about making holes in the bottom of bags so the rice falls all over the floor and—"

"Okay, okay, I get it. You couldn't possibly show yourself. You have work that's too important."

"Exactly," said Intus, satisfied. They aren't big on irony or sarcasm, in case you haven't noticed.

"Kate, you are looking exceptionally radiant today. Have you just eaten a human?" Imps aren't big on tact either. They don't see the world in quite the same way we do.

"Um, yes, and thank you. He deserved it though," Kate added hurriedly, less than comfortable with Intus' no-nonsense approach. She'll get used to it.

"Well, keep it up. It seems to be agreeing with you."

Kate looked to me for help but she was on her own. There was nothing I could do to make it better. Then something struck me. "Fancy a sandwich?"

"Love one. I thought you'd never ask," said Kate with relief.

"Have you got Marmite?" asked Intus, ears pointing forward in anticipation.

"I do. It's still in the back of the cupboard from the last time you came over."

Intus' ears pricked up and the wild tail scratched against the dashboard. Then it clapped little hands together in glee. "Then, yes, I would love a sandwich. But no bread, it bloats me, and no butter. That stuff comes from inside cows! You do know milk is a bovine excretion, don't you?" Intus asked suspiciously.

"Um, yeah. Why?"

"Why!? Because it's gross, that's why." Intus shook its pointy head in disgust at the things humans do.

"Hey! You eat Marmite. I don't think you're the one to judge me. You do know it's just yeast extract, right?"

"Hmm, yum." Intus was lost in memories of consuming yeast extract, a faraway look in the slitted eyes as it remembered the good times had with a jar of black poison masquerading as a spreadable treat for the ill-informed, or for people who couldn't afford cheese or ham.

"Okay, let's go." I started the car.

Intus jumped onto Kate, accidentally landed in her cleavage, then popped a smug head out of her blouse and said, "For safety, that's all. Spark is a reckless driver."

Kate smiled down and patted the top of the jagged head carefully. Lucky bugger.

The sneaky imp winked at me and didn't even try to bite Kate's finger for being so patronizing. If it had been me, it would have taken the top off and swallowed it.

This is a creature that gets grossed out by milk but will happily eat unwanted human flesh if it gets the point across.

Imps!

Death by Marmite

Unlocking the freshly glossed front door to my nice semi on the outskirts of the city felt odd because it felt so familiar and normal. I live in a nice, spacious house with friendly neighbors. It's quiet here. Just how I like it.

I don't have skulls hanging from beads. I don't have a collection of arcane stuff on shelves, weird creatures in jars, or a library full of magic books. There are no collections of wizard paraphernalia, or any of that stuff, and you'd be hard pressed to find a proper Hidden that does—vampires go in for the dramatic, and amass a lot of tat over the centuries and so do some wizards, but mostly it's interesting items they've picked up on their travels: a nice rug, a cushion, or a piece of furniture, not actual magical items.

In fact, there aren't usually books on magic at all. This business is strictly hands on. There is little to actually say to conjure up demons, or rituals that will guarantee results. Yes, you may get the occasional book on herb lore or low level spells, or even books on tattoos to maximize control of the Empty, but most of this world is a mind game or one where you are simply magical. The learning comes from experience, from immersion in the Empty and the feelings that grow within you, not from reading books.

And anyway, I like to keep my home simple. Clean, light and airy, and smelling nice—so sue me, I'm not a slob and I don't dress in a cape and a pointy hat.

This is the modern age. That stuff went out centuries ago, not that it was ever in with anyone that genuinely could call themselves a wizard, witch, or any other name you care to call them, or they care to call themselves.

As I opened the door, and the large open space greeted us, I breathed in deeply of the delicately scented air, the hint of rose and citrus relaxing me, welcoming me back to my own personal slice of normality.

There's nothing like coming home, especially after the kind of morning I'd had.

"Aah, home sweet home." I pushed the door to behind me.

"Looks nice," said Oliver, peering past me, eyes lingering on Kate.

"What the hell are you doing here?"

"Why, keeping an eye on you. Kate looks well. Had a nice feed did you, Kate?" he called passed me, smiling, exposing his canines.

"I thought you said he'd gone," said Kate to me, ignoring Oliver. She turned to him, but remained where she was. Intus had already gone ahead; it was probably looking for my socks. "Have you been following us?"

"Of course. I have to ensure that the mess Spark here made is cleaned up properly."

"Well it is," I said. "Now, if you don't mind?" I pushed the door but he stopped it with his foot.

"Not going to invite me in?"

"No."

"I can just come in anyway, you know?"

"And I can tell Taavi that you intruded without an invitation." It gave him pause for thought. It's where the myth of vampires not being able to enter your home unless invited comes from. All Hidden have to respect each other's homes. It's kind of off-limits unless the circumstances are very extenuating, like if you are trying to kill each other or something. To enter uninvited is like declaring war, and Oliver knew the consequences for such an act.

Taavi would be less than amused, and Oliver risked both his position and his life.

He scowled and said, "Fine, but I'm fed up chasing you around and watching you and your boring life. Give me the keys, I'll wait in the car."

"No chance." I thought for a moment. "Fine, but don't stink it up." He took the keys and left. Rikka would go mad if he knew, but it was better than wondering where Oliver was, or what he was doing.

"I don't like him. He creeps me out. He's always so smug."

"Tell me about it. He'll be gone soon, don't worry."

"Good." Kate walked back to me, grabbed my hand and squeezed, then closed the door behind us. We moved away from the door as Intus appeared in front of us in the large open plan ground floor. It tried to hide a sock, realized it was futile, then held it out and grinned happily.

When I bought the place for cash many years ago, I was well ahead of the times. It was cramped and made up of a series of poky rooms. I got rid of the lot. I took down every wall apart from the ones that actually made it a house. Gone was the wall that separated the hallway from the living room. Then I knocked through into the dining room and then the kitchen, and as the years have gone by I've modernized as new technology arrives and I'm happier with it now than I've ever been.

Stripped, polished and stained oak floorboards, the originals. A large galley kitchen at the far end overlooking the garden Grandma helped me plant and advised me on. Two large, comfortable-but-modern leather sofas either end of a rug probably worth more than the house. A huge TV on the wall, gray blinds at the bay window to the front, and a matching roller blind at the rear. Various cupboards and chairs from the forties, fifties, and sixties. It's paradise. It's mine. It's quiet. It's home.

Airy, light, roomy, and relaxing. Perfect.

"Sweet pad, Spark. Need a roomie?" asked Intus.

"Absolutely not. I like my privacy and my alone time. You ask that every time, anyway. Don't pretend like I don't remember." I tried not to shudder as Intus might take it personally. But could you imagine?

"Did I? Have I?" Long-lived creatures like Intus forget more than you would think. Or, sometimes, choose to forget on purpose. "Hey, what's this?" Intus jumped up onto a long, and very expensive forties Danish sideboard and lifted a plastic lid.

"Whoa! Don't touch it, it's set up just right. It's delicate." Intus paused with one tiny hand just about to touch the weight on the end of the needle arm of my turntable.

"You sure you don't want me to touch it. Just to be sure?"

"Sure of what?" I asked suspiciously.

"Um, to be sure it works. How does it work?"

"Never you mind. If you want that sandwich minus the bread then please don't touch my stuff."

"Fine." Intus acted seriously offended, but disappeared in a puff of smoke and reappeared on the kitchen counter, then vanished again. We heard it clattering about in the wall cupboard that held the Marmite, lost at the back where the nasty stuff remained until it began to gain sentience.

Kate shrugged and wandered down to the kitchen area. She opened the door to find Intus heaving against the jar larger than itself. Why it was in my house I had no idea. I'd certainly never bought it. One mystery that will never be solved, I guess.

She picked it up with the imp sat on the top, and I got bread out of the drawer. It was from the day before so still pretty fresh, and while I sliced, Kate got the goodies from the fridge.

"Hey, a little help here?" asked Intus, spinning the lid but not getting it off.

"I thought you were like a million times stronger than your size dictates?" I asked.

"Hey, that's sizeist. Don't be insulting me, Spark."

"What! I wasn't. Here, let me." Intus jumped down and I took off the lid and tried not to retch at the foul smell. I got a knife, loaded it up, then placed it on a plate.

Intus tucked in happily, sighing with satisfaction.

Kate and I prepared a more sensible lunch of cheese, ham, mayo and mustard sandwiches. I was starving.

Bang, bang, bang.

"What the hell is that?" I gathered the Empty, half a sandwich in my mouth, and Kate became a blur.

She was across the room quicker than you could say, "Run, vampire, run," and peeking through the blinds as the hammering at the door got louder and louder. It sounded like a troll collective had come for lunch, and I didn't expect the door to hold out much longer.

"I'm found," moaned Intus from the counter, before ducking down behind the Marmite.

"Who's found you?" Like this was what I needed now.

"Illus. You have to hide me. I've got things to do. I need a break. I need my Marmite."

"So this is why you came to see me? To hide? What's going on, Intus? I'm not in the mood for trouble today. I've got enough problems as it is."

"I thought I'd be safe with you," the cowering imp moaned, trying to whisper but its crazy imp baritone would easily be heard the other side of the door. I expected it to smash down any second. I'd just painted it, too.

"I can hear you in there, Intus. You better open up or I'll smash it down and drag you out. We have babies to make."

Kate dashed back to the kitchen and we turned to Intus. "Babies?" she said.

"Babies?" I said.

"Babies," Intus said, nodding a pale red head as it peeked around the jar.

"Who's at the door? Who's Illus?"

"My betrothed. Um, we got married."

"What!? What the hell is happening? Imps don't get married, do they?"

"Of course they do. How else would we make babies?"

"Well, you know, the same way humans and all other animals do."

"I know how to do it, thank you very much. I am immortal. I've had loads of practice, but I haven't made any yet. We can't, not until we get married. But I changed my mind, it's too... It's too—"

"Too what?" said the imp I assumed was Illus, as the angry creature squeezed through the letterbox. Seemingly, it finally remembered it was an imp, and disappeared then reappeared beside Intus, hands on hips, scowling at my terrified friend.

"Come in, why don't you?"

"Sorry about that, um, human? But we have babies to make. We're married."

"Oh, right. Er, Spark, you can call me Spark."

"Hi, Spark," said Illus. "So, this is who you've run off with, is it? Some kind of 'person.' Not good enough for you, am I?"

Intus practically shriveled before our eyes. Kate nudged me like I should do something, but I was at a loss.

"Um, who's the husband and who's the wife?" They both scowled at me like I'd asked the dumbest question ever.

"Don't be stupid," said Illus.

"Right, sorry. Daft of me to ask." They nodded in agreement. "Now, look, you, er, can't just come in here and..." Illus was seriously putting me off. The feisty imp was way too intense. I could see why Intus had done a runner.

"Yes? You got something to say?" said Illus.

"Um, no. As you were."

Intus looked at me with pleading eyes. The tail was down, ears flat to the head, and it hadn't even finished the Marmite.

"I need a break," said Intus. "It was a mistake and I'm sorry, but I'm not ready for this. It's too sudden."

"We've been engaged for seventeen centuries," said Illus.

"Like I said, too sudden. I haven't had time to prepare."

"Prepare what?"

"Um, you know, things. Married type things." Intus waved the notion away as if it were obvious such a short engagement would never result in a happy marriage.

"I think we better leave them to it," said Kate, nodding to the garden.

"Good idea."

We strolled out into the sweet smelling garden and shut the door behind us. Man, imps are loud.

After a tour of the plants, and the call of our sandwiches too much to stand, we headed back inside.

"Oh my god, oh my god," screamed Kate.

"Ugh, gross. Stop it, stop it."

It was the stuff of nightmares. All I could see was a red bottom pumping up and down at incredible speed. All blurry and red, and impish. And nasty.

Tails flew about wildly. Arms thrashed and clawed at backs and bosoms—I think they were bosoms —and moans loud enough to cause avalanches rattled the windows, and would no doubt disturb the neighbors, as the pumping got faster and the moans grew ever louder and higher in pitch.

Then it was over, and after some considerable fumbling with their brown leather dungarees and assorted buckles and bits and pieces, two imps stood and stared at us. Intus said, "What?"

"You were doing the dirty next to the Marmite. On my kitchen counter. I'll have to buy bleach!" I moaned.

"You humans are so weird," said Intus. "Can I take the jar?"

"Eh? What?"

"The Marmite?" Intus tapped the jar.

"Um, yeah, sure. Call it a wedding gift."

"Result!" said Intus, punching the air.

"Yes!" said Illus, screwing on the lid and balancing it on its head.

"Be seeing you," said Intus, waving and beaming like an imp that had just... Well, you know.

"Um, bye, then."

"Bye, humans," said Illus.

With a little puff of smoke they were gone.

"Which one was doing what?" asked Kate.

"I don't know, and I don't want to know." I stared at the forever-tainted counter and moved over to my sandwich. It had a tiny imp bumprint in the bread. "I'm not hungry."

"Me either."

Some things are scary, some things are terrifying, but there is nothing that will haunt me more than the sight of a tiny red bum going at it on my counter and ruining my lunch.

"At least they took the Marmite away," said Kate.

"Yeah. I'm gonna take a shower."

Tattoo Reveal

A foul stench launched itself at my unprepared nasal cavities as I closed the bathroom door, took off my jacket and unbuttoned my shirt. It permeated the room and overpowered the air freshener. It was me. I stank. I had the same clothes on as the day before, and assumed I hadn't washed since then either. My clothes were more wrinkled than a mummy's bandages.

Nasty.

Putting, or trying to put, images of tiny imp bums out of my mind and just have peace for a while—some me time—I stripped off the rest of my abused suit and kicked it all into a corner of my large bathroom.

Staring at myself in the mirror, I traced the lines of ink that covered my body, tattoos given long ago when I was little more than a kid. I couldn't help wonder what he would make of me now, that child. Would he be pleased? Disappointed? Awed? Probably just laugh about the imp thing, knowing me.

The tattoos are really a single tattoo, an unbroken line that starts at my left wrist and goes for a walk over my entire body. You can trace the whole thing if you want, but it would take a while.

I'm not one for runes, artifacts, or unnecessary paraphernalia for my art, but the ink is important. It matches perfectly the power lines that run through my body—some would call them chakras—that channel my energy and that of the Empty.

The combination allows me to become something more than I ever could otherwise. These are mine, personal and a part of me. The ink allows me to be who I am, and it's dangerous.

For years I fought with them. They had a life of their own, were hard to control, prone to anger, and activated at inopportune moments. Or they got carried away and sucked up more power than I needed, or made me discharge more magic than was strictly necessary—I got into a lot of trouble for my wild acts.

But over the years I gained control, and for normal lifetimes now they have been as much a part of me as breathing.

I sucked in my stomach as I examined myself in the mirror. I looked pretty good, actually. Slim, but toned and with enough muscle to be attractive, but not too much, as that would mean spending more time in the gym at Rikka's House and unofficial Council headquarters. I went a few times a week when it was quiet, just to stay in shape, and that was plenty.

The blond hair was a shock. I'd half-forgotten quite how pale I'd dyed it, but I could get used to it, and it's nice to have a change now and then. I turned on the shower, let it heat through, then stepped into the cubicle.

My thoughts moved too fast and I couldn't keep up. The day had been too intense, with too much happening. It was more than I usually saw in a week, sometimes months, and I needed some down time to gather myself back together. I knew now wasn't the time.

Once I was clean, I got dressed in a nice dark suit and the usual red shirt. Wondering what on earth could happen next, I went back downstairs.

The TV was on and Kate was sitting forward on the sofa, eyes glued to the screen.

I joined her and we sat there for ten minutes, her flicking through the news channels and both of us smiling the whole time. She'd done it. Kate had saved me.

There is no telling how happy I felt, how relieved. I had seriously panicked that I would be put down for what I'd done. Neither Rikka nor Taavi are known for their forgiveness, but if the news was anything to go by then I was well and truly off the hook.

The Grandmaster had shocked the morgue with his sudden awoken state, so straight away the news focused on what went wrong at the hospital, rather than me killing him. There were endless clips of the doctored footage Kate had let loose, and the whole thing turned more into a comedy really. The news anchors dismissed the whole incident as a prank, and the latest in a long line of manufactured-to-be-viral, online videos.

My terrible act was lost in the melee. And besides, the footage of me was far from perfect. I was almost my usual everyman, meaning my magic had still been hiding me to some extent. Nobody would recognize me if I was stood right in front of them. That's not to say the magic didn't look real, it certainly did, but so did what Kate had done. You couldn't tell what was fake and what was genuine.

I felt silly for panicking and thinking I would be picked up from the footage, but at the time I hadn't known what I was, or what I was capable of, so I forgave myself. Almost. The Grandmaster would still die, and I have to live with that. He is the first innocent I have ever killed, and it's inexcusable. And it's a shame about the hair, too.

Click.

Kate turned the TV off. We'd seen enough; I was saved. "Looks like you're in the clear."

"It sure does. Thanks, Kate. I owe you big time."

"My pleasure."

We sat in silence for a little while, but I knew I had things to do so offered to take her home. She said she would come with me, but it wasn't a good idea, so, after a few quick bites of leftovers from the fridge, my appetite recovered, I took her home.

Oliver remained quiet in the car. I knew he was itching to get Kate closer to him—she is a catch, after all—but she is Taavi's, and it meant she was to be treated with the utmost respect at all times.

Kate ignored him—she likes him about as much as I do.

We said goodbye outside the door to her building, her knowing I knew she would be back out in minutes, unable to stay cooped up with blood magic running through her veins, me not mentioning it, trying not to think of what she might get up to in her current elevated state. I left.

Time to go see Rikka again, hope he had forgiven me, and find out more about the Armenian.

Undead and Dangerous

"You took your time. I'm bored," growled Oliver as I got into the car. He was angry. Good.

"Tough. Go home and have a sleep if you don't want to be here. I honestly don't care." He glared at me.

I called ahead and was told Rikka was busy but to hang on. A few minutes later he came on the line.

"Spark, well done for sorting out the mess. I must congratulate you on a job well done."

"Um, thanks, Boss." Right away I knew he wanted something. "It's not over yet though," I added hurriedly.

He ignored me in his usual way. "I wasn't expecting you to be available so soon, but seeing as you have cleared up your troubles then I need you for this."

Damn, should have called later but it was too late now. "What do you need?" I asked warily. "I do have the Armenian to deal with, you know."

"Yes, yes, plenty of time for that. This won't take long. We have a bit of a situation and I was just putting a team together, but you will be perfect. You and a few others."

"Okay, what is it though?" I hate it when he's evasive, it always means trouble.

"The zombies. It seems they have been a little naughty. We need to go have a word, make a few minor repairs, that sort of thing."

"Zombies!" I sighed. Too late now. "Fine. Usual place?"

"Isn't it always? See you there in thirty." He hung up.

"I hate zombies," came the voice of Oliver from the rear, spitting out the word like he was some kind of prize specimen.

"Don't come then." I glanced at him in the rearview. He glared at me but said nothing. The only thing worse than having a vampire ride around with you is forgetting you have a vampire riding around with you—it makes you jump every time they open their nasty mouth.

Rikka's domain over the zombies comes with the job of being Head of the UK Dark Council—they are magic-infused beings after all. But they are so unorganized and rather forgetful that they would never think to arrange either their own Head or Council. Unsurprising, as they can't even keep their own limbs attached half the time, so what hope is there of that?

They are also a real pain and I've dealt with them on numerous occasions. I guess you could say they have a leader of sorts, although I use the term very loosely, just like their limbs and organs.

Well, I had no choice now. I was back in Rikka's good books and you don't turn him down. Ever.

Rikka is an odd guy. To look at him you just think fat, but he's a shrewd businessman, very intelligent, ruthless, more powerful at magic than anyone else I have ever met, but hardly ever uses it now as he has us for that.

He's over nine hundred years old, has seen more than I can possibly imagine, knows his way around magic like a true Hidden, and was even slim once.

Rikka is old skool in many ways, upholds traditions of magic centuries out of date, and when a young man he had his apprenticeship in a proper school for wizards back in Finland, where he wore robes and a pointy hat and even had a wand, so he told me. Those days are long gone. There are no schools now. Where would you put them? And kids won't be seen dead in a pointy hat because before they knew it it would be all over the Web and their mates would laugh at them.

Now it's all attitude and keeping up with trends, which is all for the good as magic is for the strong, not those who want to play about and turn cats into frogs or vice-versa. But Rikka remembers the old days, had serious training from many of those on the Dark Council—some much older than him—and I guess you could call the whole Council a bit of a boys club. That's right, no women.

Some traditions and institutions are a little slower to update, but the women have a strong presence on the Hidden Council and it won't be long before the wizards that dominate the Dark Council have to get with the times.

So, for all Rikka's power and fortitude, he was still nervous about dealing with whatever the zombies had been up to, which meant only one thing: the day was about to get a lot worse.

"Great, goddamn zombies." I drove out of the city and in half an hour I was at zombie headquarters. I'm not a fan, in case you haven't guessed. They're so sad, desperate to stay alive against all the odds. And bitey. Very bitey. Plus the undead are entirely unpredictable. It makes me nervous, and wish I had a scarf, but they never go with the suit.

*

Zombies have to be contained, there are no two ways about it. You can't have people wandering around loose if the first thing they will do is try to eat folk. It's just not right. So they have zones, and there are numerous such places around the country, same as all over the world. They are heavily protected with magic, lines drawn around the perimeter that stop them passing.

I've even helped with a few myself, and they have to be strong as zombies don't feel pain, will happily lose a limb or two if it means brains, and are often pretty stupid to boot. All of it means they are tricky to deal with and mostly refuse to recognize that anyone is in charge.

I took the access road to their compound, thinking it would be better to park at the side of the building then walk the rest of the way, just in case they were out of control and so I could get an idea of what had happened. Pulling up to the spot where I'd been a few times before, because of one incident or another, I checked out the woods to my right and the sloping lawns that led up to their expansive home. All clear.

I got out the car, ignored the rain, and looked down at my shoes as I heard the squelch.

"Great, just great." My winklepickers were covered in mud and that wasn't the half of it. The place was a total disaster zone. The ground was a quagmire, there were bits of goop everywhere, and Rikka hadn't arrived.

Writing off the shoes, I headed across the open ground toward their compound, but it was strangely quiet. That was a very bad sign.

"Shit, shit, shit." I nearly went over as my leg refused to move. I looked down to see a mud-covered ghoul clawing at my suit trousers with his dirty tongue licking the air, getting a taste of my magic and probably a hint of brain.

I kicked with my other leg at his hands but he held on tight, and then the mud erupted into a mass of writhing bodies and I almost panicked.

"Goddamn zombies!" They are sneaky buggers, they really are.

"Do something," I yelled at Oliver. The coward just moved past in a blur, streaking through the mud and away from the carnage in a split-second, then stood up on higher ground.

"I'm not to interfere. I'm to watch only." He grinned and I hated him more than ever.

I dismissed him as unimportant. I had more immediate concerns. The ground was alive, writhing with more limbs than at a vampire orgy, and twice as messy. They would eat me, and I'd be a real treat. Full of magic. My flesh would animate them like they'd probably never been animated before, even in life.

Bodies kept on emerging, slowly getting to their feet, slipping and sliding with their uncoordinated limbs as they gnashed their teeth and moaned for my mental matter.

The tugging on my leg increased and then there were two, pulling at me like insistent children for ice-cream, except they wanted something a lot warmer, preferably pulsing.

I seriously wasn't in the mood. Couldn't believe Rikka hadn't warned me about this, and, I admit, the anger rose a little. I looked toward the large country home that was their very nice compound, and across the neat lawns to the muddy mess I was stood in, wondering what the hell had happened.

All the while, the dark magic welled up in every cell of my body until my tattoos scratched my skin like I was wrapped in a shroud of rose thorns.

My brown eyes darkened, the whites turning black with flecks of silver that put me firmly in my Black Spark zone.

I raised my arms from my sides, lifting them and calling the Empty to me like a lover you hate with all your heart but need more than the pain it causes. Magic flowed through me and outward in a shock wave that almost sent me to my knees as the ground buckled and the mud and zombies rode a tidal wave of Empty energy, collapsing into the churned earth as rain beat down hard and my body fizzed.

They were clambering back to their feet almost instantly—that's what you get for playing nice. I didn't want to inflict more damage on the poor creatures than they already had, if I wasn't going to outright kill them then it was the height of cruelty to blast away, sending limbs flying, knowing they would continue to exist no matter what I did, short of separating them from their heads.

Admitting my sympathy, and even admiration, for the undead worked against me though, and I felt the magic dissipate, the sickness taking its place. With little choice if I wanted to escape without having a hard decision to make about my future—to be undead or permanently dead, that is the question—I focused my mind. My tattoos shone through my clothes, black and silver lines flashing like angry sparklers on bonfire night, crackling and hissing like I was nothing but a bagful of angry snakes.

Disruptive power surged hard through my body, lumpy and nasty, spreading down and up, converging at my navel. I pushed out fast with both hands, but with just a touch of mercy.

The zombies were up now, lunging for me, teeth gnashing like hungry hippos, no thought in their heads but to devour me. The force of my magic, my borrowed magic, hammered down on them like a shower of cannonballs. They crumpled like ragdolls, and the ground squashed flat like a bad landscape job, the footprints, the holes, the muddy rivulets all flattened, the undead along with them.

I kept the worst of my annoyance away from them, used just enough to make them docile and harmless, but they would certainly have one monster of a headache, if they had such feelings.

Their simple minds were quiet, shut down for a few precious moments. I wasted no time. With the magic still coursing through my veins, the sickness not yet fully upon me, I ran through the mud and bodies, not caring if I stomped on dirt, heads or limbs, and made it onto the incongruous neat lawn. I dashed up toward the building.

The ground rose as I got closer to the large house, and I collapsed onto the grass, staring back at the scene of destruction. It just looked like the usual side entrance to the compound where it met the woods, but they shouldn't have been there. It was where the pigs ordinarily went about their pig business, and was why it was so muddy. I'd seen no pigs though, although if they had any sense they would have run off the moment they caught a whiff of slowly rotting flesh.

Oliver was by my side, smiling down at me, wiggling an eyebrow. "Nasty."

"Shut up."

The sickness took me over as the magic reluctantly seeped away, leaving me shaking and empty of emotion, the terrible aftereffect of using magic all that remained, all I was.

You know when someone kicks you in the crotch and you get not only the pain, but that feeling deep inside of you as if you will never stand up straight again or breathe normally? And there is nothing else in the world but the hurt and the deep ache in places you never even knew could feel such intense sensation that is something beyond pain? Using magic for humans, especially when you use more than a hint of what it can offer, is like that feeling but in every cell of your body and brain.

You don't just hurt, ache, feel sick and incapable of doing anything but wait for death, it's so far beyond that. You become a non-person, lost in the ferocious payback for what you have done. I've been doing this for almost a hundred years and it has not once got easier—this is the price for messing with things that are not yours by birthright, and it is glorious.

Yes, as I sat there doubled up, my mind empty of everything but sorrow and anguish so deep I would gladly have given my soul to feel anything else ever again, and as my nerves fired off scream after silent scream to my brain that couldn't cope with so many dark and mean signals from every part of my being and yet refused to shut down totally, part of me, the addicts part, reveled in the power and the sheer intensity of such emotion and feeling. Once more, I was lost to magic.

It sounds nuts, I know. Why would you want to go through such torment? But the power overwhelms you even more than the sickness, and something tells you that in a moment it will pass—not that it feels like it—and that you are something more than human. You are elemental, invincible, and dangerous as hell. Powerful. It corrupts you and you love it and you hate it and you want it to end and you want it to last for eternity.

My breathing slowed as the pressure of insanity receded. My body became my own and my mind cleared.

"No feeling like it, am I right?" Oliver was on a stolen high. His blood lust had risen with my use of magic, a taste for him of the blood magic, the sickness, and the power vampires got from their own perverse twisting of such energies. He was itching for more.

"Shut up. Leech."

I stood, breathing deep of the country air. All that remained were the after-effects, the magic high that was mine and mine alone. Part of who I am, who I will always be.

The zombies were still all down, only moving slightly. They would be that way for a few minutes more.

What the hell was going on?

"Hey, Spark, I see you've been busy."

Turning, I smiled my best smile. "Hey, Plum. Nice day for it, isn't it?"

"You found them, then?" she said, ignoring my winning smile, and the practically salivating Oliver, nodding at the zombies.

"I didn't know they were missing, not that many. What's going on?"

"Exactly that. Paul lost the zombies so he called Rikka, but I guess you found them for him."

"Yeah, I guess I did."

Paul the Zombie

Plum hauled me to my feet as though I were made of air. I stopped to admire the muscles and the curves—she does wear her outfits tight—and gave her my best, most lovely of smiles. She stared at me with that look she has, like she is all business and what is wrong with you?

Undeterred, I kept at it. If nothing else I am persistent. I cocked my head to one side and waited. There was no question, it was coming.

"Idiot," she said, and laughed. She punched me playfully on the arm and I nearly went down again.

"Hey, if we can't smile then it might as well all be over."

"Idiot," she repeated, smiling. Her smile is beautiful, so is she, and I lust after her and always have.

But you know what? I wouldn't any more go to bed with her than I would one of the zombies. Why? Because of Kate. But also because of the panther thing. Shifters are dangerous, very dangerous, and they stick to their own kind. It's a prerequisite really, totally understandable.

When they get excited, or angry, or just will it to happen, then they shift, and you don't want to be caught naked and helpless in a room with a horny panther. At least I don't think so.

So I admire from afar, or as close as I can risk without getting a slap, but we both know it's just flirting, and that makes it all the better. It's fun. No danger of claws or teeth getting involved.

Still, she is hot. Oh-so-hot, and the tight leggings and vest she wore meant she knew it—it was my problem if I couldn't handle it.

I'm Dark Magic Enforcer, Black Spark, Conqueror of Smokin' Ladies. I can handle a little sexiness. Gulp.

"Ah, Spark, I wondered when you would turn up," said Rikka, stood next to a few goons, with Paul the zombie a respectable distance away from anyone living. Rikka had a few trolls around him, with another next to Paul. Trolls are perfect when on zombie business—they can't bite through the rock, although they still sometimes try. His face darkened when he caught sight of Oliver. The vampire had the sense to nod in greeting, but remain silent.

"What! I've been here a while, where were you?"

"We came through the front, like civilized people," said Rikka, staring at me, bemused.

We wandered around to the front of the building and stood on the gravel drive. I noticed the cars the other side of the large fountain that took center stage in a sweeping sea of pebbles.

"Yeah, well, I thought it best to come the back way just in case. Seems I found your lost zombies, Paul. What happened?"

"I was just explaining it to Mage Rikka when we heard the commotion," said Paul, putting a hand to his jaw to click it back into place—it did that a lot. A sure sign of age and zombie sickness, one of the drawbacks to being undead.

"Well, how about you fill me in, too. Are there any other nasty surprises?"

"There's no need for that, Spark. They are people, you know. Unlike him." Paul scowled and pointed at Oliver loitering by the cars, looking bored, feigning disinterest. Rikka had chosen to ignore him altogether. Lucky for me, he hadn't asked how Oliver arrived. Otherwise he'd be sniffing the SUV like a trained hound.

"Um, okay." I shook off the aftereffects of the Empty and pulled myself together, straightened my jacket, ruffled my hair, and tried not to look at my shoes and trousers. I'd be billing Rikka, no doubt.

"It seems we had another outbreak, but I had no idea until just now how bad it was," wheezed Rikka, clearly wishing he had a chair.

It's always odd seeing him out from behind his desk and away from the gym. He never seems quite as fat—like a slimline version of himself he puts on for trips. He was by no means slender looking, but he seemed more alive, a hint of the man he really was. Powerful beyond compare and more dangerous than a pack of panther shifters in a chicken shed.

When I see him like that I understand why he is Head of both the UK Hidden and Dark Councils—he oozes magic and power more than he oozes sugar and grease.

"Oi," grunted Stone, the troll next to Paul. Stone is small by troll standards, only half the size of a house rather than a full one. Still huge, in other words.

"Oh, sorry. I do apologize, Stone. Old habits, I'm afraid." Paul put his jaw back again and stepped away from Stone. He'd gone in for a bite, getting nothing but a lick of mineral-enriched rock for his trouble.

"Watch it. Stone understand though. Got hunger."

"Yes, well, this is all very nice and everything," said Mage Rikka, "but if this is all, Paul, we will be on our way. I trust you can clean up the mess out there?"

"Yes, of course. But could you, you know, strengthen the barrier a little? My comrades seem to be getting a little unruly of late. I don't know what's got into them." Paul looked worried, more worried than usual, and I couldn't blame him. He had an unenviable job on his hands.

"Fine, I shall do my best. Shall I bring it in a little, to ensure the pigs stay safe? If they haven't been eaten, that is."

"Oh, yes please, Mage Rikka. Although, they will be fine, I am sure. Probably off in the woods snuffling about like pigs do."

"Hmm. Maybe some refreshments then, while we wait for you to clean up a little. Get your, er, people back into the grounds. Yes?"

"Absolutely," beamed Paul through green teeth —those he still had. He signaled to his staff and I tried not to groan out loud. He shuffled away at the usual zombie pace—this would take a while.

"What happened here? I've never known this many of them to get out before. Sneaky buggers were lying in the mud." It was odd behavior. Usually they'd be wandering about all dazed like, arms out in front, doing the usual moaning bit and making you feel sorry for them.

"Seems the guards kind of forgot about them, didn't put them in last night. The poor things must have been after the pigs so ended up down in the mud. Paul needs to get his act together or I'll replace him." Rikka isn't really a fan of having to deal with things like this himself, but it comes with the job and if he wants to maintain his position, as he has for a very long time, then he has to get his hands dirty now and then.

"Paul's getting on a bit now, but he's a good guy," I said. "He might just need a vacation."

"Maybe, we'll see. For now, let's just go relax and wait for them to get the zombies back inside."

Rikka's eye twitched as he stared at Oliver for a moment, then turned and walked toward the entrance to the building. It had once been a luxury spa resort but the Dark Council had taken it over to make a zombie enclave. They deserved some comfort, even if it was little more than a prison.

We walked through the open doors into the cool interior, and I couldn't help but marvel at the marble floor. It's amazing. Massive tiles laid out in a simple black and white abstract pattern, but somehow coming together to make something stunning. It's kind of wasted on the zombies.

As we entered, Paul came from one of the large rooms with a number of more together—they had all limbs and features—undead, and they left to herd their fellow kind back up to the building.

We went into the dining room and myself, Rikka, and Plum sat at the table and admired the spread Paul had laid on—food was a prerequisite of such a visit by Rikka, everyone knew that. You didn't forget if you valued his help, his protection, his magic.

"Please, help yourselves," said Rikka, stuffing a sandwich into his mouth and slurping tea.

I didn't need asking twice. Dark magic use really takes it out of you, not to mention the adrenaline rush that depletes your energy like a cave-man comedown. I'd also cut my lunch short, for obvious red bum reasons.

Rikka nodded at me appreciatively as I munched on the sandwiches and absolutely did not think about what meat the zombie kitchen staff had used—they wouldn't use human meat, as they would see that as a waste, but when invited to lunch by the immortal-until-you-rot undead you can't blame a guy for feeling a little anxious.

"You did well, Spark."

"Thanks, Rikka. I had a little help."

"Yes, I heard from Dancer. He seemed to have enjoyed himself. It's always good to keep your hand in. Er, not too deep, though."

I wasn't sure what he meant by that, and didn't ask. "Yeah. He's not so bad. He did well, actually. Real pro job."

"Dancer may be many things, but an amateur he is not. So, the Grandmaster lives, for now, and that takes the heat off. And the other stuff, the Internet and video thing, very inventive. I assume it wasn't all your idea, or work?"

Like he didn't know. Rikka likes to play his little games, but they always lead somewhere. Always.

"No. Kate helped me out. She saved me, saved all of us."

"From the mess you caused." Rikka held up a fat hand to stop me interrupting. "Yes, I know, it wasn't your fault. It was the..." He paused to check for eavesdroppers. "Armenian's fault."

Plum's eyes went wide at the mention of the name, and looked at me with sympathy. Everyone had heard of the Armenian, but why was I the one that had to deal with her? I obviously hadn't done a good job of it first go around.

"Exactly. Anyway, crisis averted. The way all the fake videos are gaining traction online nobody will think anything of my mistake. Job done."

"Not quite."

"The Armenian?" Rikka nodded. "What exactly has she done? I know you said she did the 'thing,' but what exactly?"

"Later." Rikka stuffed another sandwich into his mouth. When he finished chewing he said, "I don't like that vampire being with you, Spark. I am in charge around here, and the whole damn country. I don't need my people being spied on like criminals. I assume this is Taavi's doing?" It had happened before, and it never ended well, but I was surprised it had taken Rikka so long to bring the subject of Oliver up.

"Yes, he insisted. I don't like it either, and he is seriously winding me up, but I couldn't say no."

"Of course not." Rikka understood, but he hated that the vampires ignored his Council, thinking they were above such things and refusing to acknowledge they were grouped under the Dark Council, seeing themselves as above human concerns.

"Taavi did say that if Oliver stepped out of line then he would pretty much wash his hands of him. He's an observer only, to ensure that everything gets covered up."

"Then he should be gone. You have done your job well. And I give you my permission, Spark."

"Your permission?"

"Yes." Rikka said no more, but I knew what he meant.

If I got the chance, and had a decent enough excuse, I was to send that sucker somewhere dark and nasty, preferably for eternity. I nodded. Rikka really hated Oliver. If I could, then I would help to put the foul man down. Taavi wouldn't be happy, but there would be nothing he could do.

We stood, as Paul and a few rather muddy and abashed zombies followed him into the dining room, making a right mess of the floor.

"Our people are contained. Would you care to do the honors, Mage Rikka?"

"If I must," sighed Rikka. We followed Paul back out the way we had come.

Magic time.

Less a Prison, More a Safe-Zone

Zombies, or the living dead, or undead, as they prefer to be known, aren't nasty, they just don't know any better. It's a timeless virus as old as magic itself, and the Hidden ensure that humanity survives by keeping them contained.

They are mostly happy for this service, as the last thing they would want is to be told they'd put an end to the world and there would never be a chance of brains or fresh flesh ever again.

The infected become something otherworldly, primordial, magical, another part of the dark magic that thrums across the universe and permeates us all.

But somehow, somewhere, some time, somebody did something very wrong, and the cosmic karma played a nasty joke to put us in our place. This original zombie, whoever he or she was, paid the ultimate price for whatever indiscretion they performed. Or maybe it was simply a virus and nobody was to blame, but either way the infection spread with a bite, and the result of a zombie getting its teeth into your skin is immortality.

Being infected does not result in a "Isn't life great, and now I get to have incredible strength and can captivate people and do whatever the hell I want" kind of immortality that vampires have, but the "I'm scared and alone, and all I crave is fresh flesh and bits of me keep falling off" immortality.

Once infected, their bodies are animated corpses, controlled by the virus as the corruption of magic overpowers them, claims them as its own. There is no escape, only a second death through utter destruction of the brain and the removal of it from the skull, or the smashing of it to a nasty pulp.

Well, a lot of them would rather not have their brains smeared across the first available surface, which is understandable, so instead they try to behave. Only problem is, that's not so easy with the overwhelming desire to eat other humans, or anything else that's still breathing if your options are limited. This means that while they are still with it enough to decide, many opt for the compounds. The safe-zones, as we prefer to call them. It sounds less like a prison.

Newly turned are almost wholly aware, just locked inside this creature drawn to human flesh like an imp to your new pair of socks. Yes, they get unstoppable cravings for other humans, but they are still the person they were, if rather pale. The color is understandable, but quickly degenerates, as without blood flowing it pools at the extremities, giving horrendous swollen features and limbs. These unfortunate creatures are animated, but very much dead.

Their solution is to drain out the blood and transfuse a special blend of preserving agents, much like a mortician would do to keep a corpse fresh, or a taxidermist to preserve their art for posterity.

But you don't exactly look your best, and mirrors aren't popular among the living dead.

Other than that it can be life as normal, but you may never go home, never see friends or family again. It has to be kept secret for obvious reasons. There are issues of health, not to mention survival of the human species.

Over many years, and countless persecutions and misunderstandings, agreements have been made between those that act as sometime leaders for the numerous zombie factions and the Hidden—it's all very amenable.

They don't want to wipe out humanity, but many prefer to remain undead than to accept the rather more permanent alternative. They have their compounds, and in each Ward the Head is responsible for the zombies, just like all other aspects of dark magic use by those classified as human, or once-human, Hidden.

It gets complicated. I think half the time nobody really knows who is in charge of what, but for the most part it all seems to work out somehow.

Rikka has charge of this enclave as it is in his local Ward, but the whole country is his too—both human Hidden and true Hidden—so it's no wonder he eats too much. As he is the most powerful, and the one the zombies trust, he deals with the magic that keeps them from turning the UK into the Apocalypse.

They'd obviously got a little carried away though, and the bind hadn't held—probably as it was old and needed updating anyway—and the pigs that act as their food had clearly tempted them too much by straying close to the edge of the magic barrier, and they'd managed to push on through then probably forgot what they were doing or where they were and had a lie down. Zombies tire easily, especially the old ones.

I can't imagine a worse existence. Watching the years pass by while you slowly rot, even with the preservatives inside you. Bits breaking off, no way to feel any of it as your nerves no longer function, body getting eaten by bugs while skin peels away. All the while somehow sure that letting it carry on for years, or decades, is worth it. Credit where credit's due, they are hardcore and no mistake.

Down at the edge of their designated area, Rikka prepared to update the magic containment line that ran around the whole area, a forcefield that stopped them crossing. A simple summoning of the Empty when done on a small scale, but for a large barrier like this Rikka was the man for the job.

Trolls, shifter, dark magic enforcer, vampire, and zombies stood well back as Rikka edged forward and did what he does best—it's a sight to behold and like the northern lights on crack.

He paused and turned back to us. "Wait in the house," he said, staring at Oliver.

"You can't tell me what to—" Rikka took a single step toward him. "Fine, fine. Didn't want to see your little show anyway." Oliver turned and walked slowly back up toward the building where he leaned against the wall and continued to push his luck.

"Definitely got to go," said Rikka, staring at me now. I nodded. He turned back to his task.

Rikka, somewhat unassuming overweight man with casual clothes and long, thin brown hair—his only concession to the days of his youth—spread his legs a little to root them properly in the earth and make a good connection, then opened his arms out wide.

His meaty arms practically blinded us as his faded ink of centuries ago bulged and vibrated rapidly, faster and faster as the air cracked and reality faded quicker than a single chuckle after a bad joke.

The world took on new and darker meaning as he drew the Empty into himself, let it envelop him by force of will and the connection he'd mastered over the ages.

He became something altogether different. Gone was the fat man, here were a thousand different Rikkas, blinking on and off like flicking through the pages of a book.

All the versions of him there had ever been and maybe ever would be, morphing from a child, to a boy, to a young man, to the man he is today, from slender novice wizard with long hair and robes, to all manner of strange incarnations as he flipped through the various body forms and styles of the centuries as if trying to find one that would fit.

The whispers of the truth behind the veneer of reality grew more intense and the Empty poured into him as his hair stood on end and his ink went wild. The power flowed, dangerous and deadly to a lesser practitioner, changing him into something primitive and pure. Energy, magic that constitutes the building blocks of all realities and was inside of him, and outside of him, and was him, and everything else, and was his to do with as he pleased.

Carefully squatting, Rikka put a finger to the grass and mumbled something unintelligible, then the finger of his other hand, while darkness whispered to him and he fought the sickness and beat it.

He slid his hands across the grass, wide and impossibly fast.

CRACK.

The ground erupted into blinding fire as dark as soot. In either direction a black line of scorched grass no thicker than his plump fingers raced away. Moments later, a less intense *crack* could be heard directly behind us on the other side of the building as the lines met.

Rikka got to his feet, turned and smiled at us, his eyes black and wide, sparks of blue catching the gray of the clouds, dangerous and masterful. Then the sickness came, even for Rikka. His smile turned to pain.

In a moment it passed and Rikka was Rikka again.

"Right, time for a quick bite to eat, then we should be off." Rikka held out an arm. Stone took it and guided him back up the slope to the house.

That's Rikka for you. He's pretty matter-of-fact about his abilities, and this was little more than an interlude to his feasting. For anyone else they would have been sick for days if they could even manage it— most couldn't. I could, but boy would I have puked.

This is why Rikka holds so much sway over human and true Hidden alike—he truly is like an elemental force of nature and I'd seen him put down demons between bites of a chocolate bar. His powers are immense but he has little in the way of forgiveness, even less remorse.

I followed them back up to the house. It would be rude to leave now, and besides, I felt sick from the magic residue. So did Paul and Plum, judging by the way they walked, although it was hard to tell with Paul —he alway staggers about and looks a little green.

My stomach sank even deeper into my dirty winklepickers as the memory that we hadn't got around to discussing what the deal was with Ankine Luisi surfaced like a soul eater and clutched at my insides—I knew the feeling wouldn't let go until I dealt with it once and for all.

Sometimes, just sometimes, I wish I'd become a baker, or a postman, or maybe even a deeply contagious virus tester. They all seemed safer ways to earn a living at that moment.

An Admission

"Ankine Luisi," began Rikka—god, how I hate that woman's name—"has overstepped her boundaries and must be stopped."

"She's never known any boundaries, that's always been the trouble."

"Exactly."

I waited for Rikka to continue but he just ate. Was that it? "So, what did she do, exactly? I know she's done 'the thing' but who with? I want details, specifics, if I'm going to pull this off."

Rikka leaned back and stared at me with eyes so old it felt like the complete history of wizardry was held within his gaze. Telling of the power that was his to call upon and the things he had seen and done. He wasn't even too troubled after the magic given to the zombies —powerful almost beyond compare. "She picked the wrong person this time, and she has to be stopped. Look, Spark, I've already been over all this with you yesterday."

"I know, but I don't remember. Most of the day is fuzzy, just like this morning. I was just there, at the table playing chess. I don't know what I did or what happened before that. After all these years of us playing, and now it's ruined." I loved chess, I truly did.

"Then I suggest you find out. Don't you think that's a good idea? And you'll get over it. The game's still there, waiting for when you are ready."

"Thanks. And I will find out what happened. But come on, give me something. What did you tell me yesterday? This is for you as well as me, you know? It's in all our best interests I have as many facts as possible."

He knew I was right, so stopped eating and stared at me, hard. Those eyes, so full of knowledge, and power, and pain. I do like Rikka, and I guess I love him. He's been part of my life for so long he's like a father, but he's distant, hard to connect with, nearly always all about business. So what he said really surprised me, and it meant more than he will ever know. Or maybe not. Maybe he knew I needed it. Maybe he did too.

"I never had children, Spark, never saw the point, or wanted the inconvenience, until you came to me and I took you under my wing. We have been through a lot together, you and I, and for a century you have been a constant in my life. Sometimes a thorn in my side, sometimes a joy to watch, but there, and I've even worried about you at times."

This was unheard of. Rikka never spoke like this. Even after all these years I had never had put into words what he felt of our relationship, and I often thought I was just another one of his people, even though I knew he had gone out of his way to help me, and my family, a very long time ago. I stared, didn't say a word. I don't think I even breathed.

"People come and go, so do other species. Most are flaky no matter their origin, and many are downright nasty, magic or no magic, but you, you are a good man, Spark. So be careful, okay?" Rikka wiped at his eyes with a napkin—I sat there with my mouth open.

I felt like a baby, how it must be when you are wrapped up in a blanket by your mum and all you feel is warmth and love and safe.

"I will. Thank you, Mage Rikka. I love you."

"You silly sod, pass me a sandwich."

I passed him two and after a few grunts and some manly eye-dodging, until we got our acts together, he finished his snack and settled back to tell me the story.

The sounds of zombies being batted away by trolls at the entrance to the dining room faded away, as did the shouting and despairing of Paul as he repeatedly had to steer the undead either inside or outside, depending on who needed fresh air and who needed to go lie in a dark room.

Plum stood to attention by the doors out to the grounds, keeping watch and acting like she wasn't eavesdropping. All that remained was me and Rikka, a man I owed my life to and a man I sometimes hated, sometimes loathed, sometimes ridiculed behind his back, but always loved.

Ankine Luisi's Tale

"You know her history, right?" I nodded. "She's as old as time, Spark. Maybe older. You think of me and even Taavi as old, and he is a lot older than me, but it's nothing. A blip. Meaningless. Even some on the Dark Council are millennia older than him or I, and we are but still children. Imps, trolls, fae, elves, the true Hidden, they are the ancient ones. Creatures of the world, or the world behind this facade we find ourselves raging against, at any rate."

"Magical creatures."

"Yes. Magic was here long before humans, and will be long after we are gone. It's why it hurts so much, but you know this. It isn't our place, not really, but we are human so, as usual, we force the issue. Such is life. Our nature is to push the boundaries, and you can't blame us for wanting to use magic any more than you can blame a troll for eating chalk."

"Haha, they do love that stuff."

Rikka ignored me—he was on a roll. "And in ages past, the succubi, and incubi, have always thrived when mankind thrived. More people, more superstition and magic, always meant more of their kind. They have many names in many cultures. Qarînah in Arabic folklore, Yakshini in India, the list goes on. Succubi are always depicted as beautiful, voluptuous women who take what they want from men in their dreams, or by their power over the weak minds of males. Ring any bells?" Rikka smirked at me.

"Yeah, maybe," I mumbled.

"Of course, they are all just stories, but as with all myths they are based on the truth. Ankine—"

"You gonna be long? I got stuff to do." Oliver leaned against the dining room door, smirking. Plum was next to him in a flash, ready to fight to the death if need be.

"Get out. NOW!" Rikka would put up with a lot, but failing to show respect for the man he was, not just his position, would never be tolerated. Especially by what he saw as nothing but the lackey of a truly evil creature.

Oliver bowed and left. "Touchy," he said, reappearing for a second.

"He's got to go. I mean it, Spark."

"I know." Like my day wasn't bad enough already.

"Now, as I was saying. Ankine Luisi is an ageless succubus. She has known many names and many countries. Has known countless men and given birth to innumerable children. But, for us, and for as long as anyone from either Council can remember, she has been the Armenian. She has always done as she wishes, and nobody dares try stop her as she cannot be stopped. Until recently Armenia remained her home."

"Shame she didn't stay there."

"That was good for us, but not good for them. You have to take a global view of things these days. No country is isolated any more, and it makes life a lot harder for us all. But it is what it is. For years now, hundreds, she has roamed the world, locked to this realm. She has visited us for so long that she is now part of it. She belongs here and cannot just come and go as she pleases and appear in men's dreams then vanish.

"Those times are long behind her, have been for centuries. She is locked out of the true Hidden world. She stayed here too long, too often, and this is how she survives now—as a physical entity that has to obey the laws of travel. I hear she even eats and drinks now. Even has an interest in fashion and home decor if you can believe it. Such is the modern age."

"Rikka, I know all this. I know what she is. What I want to know is what she has done."

"My dear boy, have patience. Indulge me. It's important you know the details."

"Sorry, Rikka." He was covering old ground, but maybe it was just his fatherly instinct—which I was amazed at him for sharing—rearing up and wanting to ensure I could be as safe as possible.

"We, the Council, none of us normally know where she is or what she is doing. She is secretive, moves like a ghost, and one minute she is mixing with royalty in some unheard of small European country, looking like she will be the next Queen, the next she pops up living a seemingly normal life as a secretary in some city or other. She gets bored, craves new experience. New men. She is still entirely a magical being, but she remains here, in physical form, showing her true self only to the man she has chosen."

"And you sent me to deal with her. Goddamn!"

"Only because I knew you could. Or at least convince her to stay away from the man she currently has enthralled and under her control."

About time. "Who is this guy? Why now? She's been around forever, as you say, so why the urgency now?"

"Because, my dear boy, she has taken a shine to Mage Teppo Quimby, Ambassador of the Finnish Dark Council, next expected Head, and both Councils are less than happy about the situation. Neither her impertinence, nor his foolishness to be so easily enamored by the likes of her. It does not bode well for his future, even if you extricate him from this mess, but it bodes even worse for him, and us all, if this continues much longer. Who knows what he has told her already. It doesn't bear thinking about."

"Blimey." In other company I would have used a strong expletive, but in many ways Rikka is a throwback to times long gone, and he will not abide what he calls base language. It's not in his nature to use vulgar vocabulary when he still revels in the joy of language and all it has to offer. I think he can speak almost every language there is, so refuses to accept swearing as part of a modern and educated person's conversation.

"Yes, blimey, indeed. Teppo and I go way back. Way, way back. I've known him for centuries and he is a good man, if a little wayward now and then. Teppo is an accomplished mage, with strong connections to the Empty, and he is from the homeland. But, and this is strictly between us, Spark," I nodded, "he is not Head material, and this proves it. He is too wild and reckless. Never thinks enough about business, and has repeatedly failed to do as he is told by his Council or the Hidden Council. He thinks he knows best sometimes, and he likes to drink and party. He's probably blown his entire career. Almost seven hundred years and he still hasn't learned how to act like a grown-up. Well, it is a shame, but you were sent to bring him to me, so I could arrange his passage home and give him a talking to."

"A talking to?" This did not bode well for Teppo. A talking to from Rikka, with all Council's agreement, was not something you wanted.

"Yes, a talking to." Rikka stared at me with those eyes of his, those intelligent, fat, sunken eyes wise beyond even his nine hundred years, and had to say no more. We both knew what it meant and it would not be good for Teppo.

"You were to go get him, and deal with Ankine Luisi."

"Oh, so just another enforcer job?" I said, wishing I had never woken from my dream-state of the morning that already felt like a lifetime ago.

"No, Spark, definitely not. This is important. To me, to you, to all of us. Why do you think I chose you?" I stared at him blankly. He sighed at my ineptitude. "Because you're the best, Faz Pound, that's why. You act like a right idiot at times, you and your suits, and your wisecracks, but you are the best enforcer I have ever had. I trained you."

"Wow! Um, thanks."

"So don't blow it twice," he said, leaning forward and staring at me. "There will be no more chances after this, Spark. I won't be able to protect you if you fail. This is out of my hands, an international affair, and there is no way the Council, or the vampires, will let you off. They won't care about the consequences. Taavi will punish you for failing, for leaving unfinished business that you have been tasked with. You know how it works."

I knew how it worked all right. If you were given a job it was your job. It didn't matter who else got involved, or how you dealt with it, as long as you abided by our rules. The only thing that mattered was the job got completed. There are records, there are Laws, there are many things we can do, but there is no forgiveness. There is certainly no mercy.

"I think I'll get going now. Lots to do, people to see, wizards to save and succubus to capture."

"That's my boy. And he's a mage, Spark, a mage." Rikka gave me a weak smile and put his half-eaten sandwich back down on the plate. I hadn't realized things were quite that serious until then. "Don't forget your sidekick," warned Rikka.

"I won't."

I left. I even forgot to ogle Plum. It was becoming a habit.

As I dodged wayward undead and made my way back to the car where I could see Oliver waiting, I wondered what to do about the vampire. Rikka had made his instructions clear, and it was unlike him, as usually he did what he could to maintain the peace.

It's always a delicate balancing act with the vampires as they are so hot-headed and prone to acting before thinking. Rikka usually keeps well out of their way as there is nothing to be gained from becoming embroiled in their business. And besides, they will have nothing to do with the Dark Council, thinking it beneath them, having their own Vampire Council, with Taavi as its Head.

They have their rules, the rest of us have ours, but all creatures of magic follow a few basic Laws that have remained unchanged for as long as anyone can remember. You stay Hidden, you do not interfere with the business of other races or species, and the Hidden Council has final say. Always.

Even Taavi acknowledges the Hidden Council. If he and other Heads throughout the world didn't, well, vampires would be wiped off the planet quicker than you could say sorry.

For Rikka to basically tell me to eliminate Oliver was pushing the boundaries a little. It would cause friction unless I had an extremely good reason for interfering.

As I got to the car I changed my mind. Oliver sneered at me in that condescending way he has, like he was better than me—all too common with vampires— and I would have happily blasted him to hell right there and then if I thought I could get away with it.

"Get in. I've got business to attend to."

"Hurry up, I'm hungry."

"Tough. Not my problem."

"It will be if you don't get your troubles sorted soon."

I turned to Oliver and got in his face. "If you threaten me ever again, I mean ever, I will rip that smug smile right off your face and feed you to the zombies piece by little piece. Do I make myself clear?"

Oliver showed his fangs and sneered again.

I got in the car. He got in behind me. I can tell you now, having a vampire sat behind you is seriously freaky. It makes the hairs on your neck stand on end and it's really hard to focus on your driving.

I ignored him best I could and headed back into the city.

A Coffee Break

"Me again. Fancy grabbing a coffee? I can make up for earlier." I didn't expect her to say yes, but it was worth a shot.

"Sure, sounds nice. Not that I was trying to have a sleep or anything."

"Oh! Whoops, sorry. I thought you would be out and about, um, burning off a little, er... Sorry."

"Burning off some what?"

"Nothing, my mistake. The usual? I'm back in town after a little diversion."

"Sure, give me fifteen minutes and I'll see you there. Is you-know-who still there?" I could almost hear the shudder.

I glanced over at Oliver who was scowling at the people walking by like they were dirt. More than anything, I hate the condescending attitude many older vampires have. It's as if they forget they were once human too. I tried not to think about Kate and what she might become. I had faith in her. I knew, and still know, that she is better than that. "Yeah, but just ignore him. I do."

"I'll try, but he's bad news, Faz. And he leers."

"Tell me about it. You still coming?"

"Sure. Get me a caramel macchiato. I fancy something different."

"Um, okay. Bye." She hung up. I had no idea what a caramel macchiato was, and still don't. These coffee shops freak me out. I always just end up ordering a filter coffee. It's like I've missed out on lessons that everyone else in the world has taken.

A cappuccino this, a dolce latte whatever. Flat whites, macchiatos and mochas—the words make me shudder. Whenever I look at the menu board in these places I'm struck dumb and then some guy or girl, who call themselves a barista, whatever that is, will ask what I want and I say coffee and feel all eyes turn to me like I'm from another planet.

How did everyone else learn this stuff? I just want something hot and strong.

I was amazed Kate wasn't off doing who-knows-what after her feed, but I guess I underestimated her and should have known she wouldn't be running around half-crazed, hyped up on blood magic and maybe skipping through an orgy of vampires, naked and covered in fluids too numerous to mention.

Loitering outside until she came felt like a very good idea. Screw ordering, I would wait, and the Champion Slayer of Demons, Mighty Wielder of Infinite Power, Puncher of the Hidden, Slapper of the

Silly, and Stutterer at Sexy Vampire Friends could have a girl get him a coffee.

I also had an ulterior motive.

After a quick trip home to change, leaving Oliver the Glum waiting outside, and a few unanswered calls to the Finnish Embassy, followed by a little over-the-phone enforcer charm of the ever-so-slightly magical kind, I managed to trace who had been working there and dealing with the day-to-day running of the place.

It took a while, as I had to go through several contacts, eventually ending up talking to one of our Hidden agency people—hey, we all have to earn a living—and convinced her to give me the number of the woman who used to work there. The name sounded familiar.

I was right. It was a Cardiff girl I'd met a few times before. One of us. Hidden. She was a young witch, still learning the ropes, and it would be many years before she could truly take the title. But Grandma knew of her and liked her, and I'd met her there a few times when I'd popped in, retreating as quickly as I could when confronted with a kitchen full of women arguing over the relative merits of St. John's Wort as opposed to whatever the alternative is—I zone out at such talk.

Those kind of get-togethers are not for the likes of me. A room crammed full of ancient women, some fun, others as serious as a vampire who hasn't fed for a century, all with a bunch of young, wide-eyed girls at various stages of learning, is enough to make the most hardened of enforcers go weak at the knees and hightail it before they can force-feed you potions—because it will do you good—or ask once again why you don't settle down and get married. And would I like to meet their granddaughter, she is quite pretty.

Anyway, Mary was a nice girl, and more than happy to tell me what she knew. She was seriously annoyed at how she had been treated, and I promised to put in a good word for her with Grandma if she could help me out. She gushed at the offer, as getting on Grandma's radar is no small matter, especially for a young witch-in-training.

It seemed that it was a regular thing for Ankine to go shopping before she and the Ambassador hit the clubs late in the evening, him hardly ever making an appearance until late the following day. Mary had received her marching orders from Teppo, who she said had begun to act strangely, but it wasn't her place to say anything. Her tone made it clear she was less than impressed with Ankine Luisi. She told me all she could about their usual routine. I just hoped that it was still the same.

I needed something to go on though, and this was the best I could come up with apart from just confronting her head on. A little intel wouldn't hurt, and I wanted to speak to Teppo alone if I could. According to Mary, Ankine was usually out until well past five, sometimes six, so I had plenty of time to see her in action, maybe get an idea of what I faced, and to be honest I suppose I was putting off the inevitable.

Pretending to talk on my phone, so I didn't look like a total loser, even though I knew Regulars couldn't even see me, only Hidden—and I bet most don't know how to get a coffee either—I watched people come and go from the stores.

We were on the main stretch through the shopping district, and most people have to pass that way to hit up the various department stores and boutiques. It was pleasant. Normal.

The rain had stopped, making the new paving gleam like a polished crystal ball as the sun made a risky move. It dared to shine for a few brief moments, before a concerted attack by the Welsh cloud gang took back their territory. The victorious clouds celebrated with a downpour so sudden and fierce the street emptied in seconds. The coffee shop risked expelling those without sufficient knowledge of its secret language as it became increasingly crowded.

Oliver scowled at the rain, but remained in the street, getting more morose the wetter he got. I acted sensibly and stood under the canopy while people came and went with their drinks and muttered about the weather like it was a revelation it rained in Cardiff.

Okay, I chose a coffee shop just to annoy Oliver. I knew he would have to remain some distance away as he had little choice if he wanted to stay alive. Vampires can't handle being in close proximity to a lot of humans, not the older ones like Oliver. It's too much temptation, like putting a witch in a herb garden and telling her to not even smell the leaves. Young ones can handle it as they don't have the same urges, but older vampires can never get enough blood magic. Even Oliver was intelligent enough to know that sitting in a crowded room would send him spiraling out of control, or make him too sick to remain.

So it was with great pleasure that I smiled at Kate when she arrived, opened the door to the unknowable world of coffee, and ushered her in ahead of me.

I winked at Oliver as we left him outside like a dog on a piece of string. Served him right.

Hopefully the bait would work.

False Pretenses

I tricked Kate into ordering coffee as I said I needed a pee, and when I returned she had picked a table in the middle of the crowded room. That wouldn't do at all. So, while she watched, bemused by this everyman, this entirely forgettable, nobody-remembers-what-he-looks-like man, I went and stood by a table at the window.

Some guy was there with a coffee and his laptop, taking up a table meant for two, coat on the empty chair and his attention lost to his Facebook timeline. I stood there, behind him, just for a second. His timeline was full of mentions of the viral campaigns Kate had put together and he laughed and tutted at the videos. Man, she had saved my hide with that.

He felt my presence and turned, then went straight back to his screen. I was nothing to look at. He would have already forgotten I was there, would never remember me, even with the bleached hair.

I let my tattoos tingle, not enough to make me feel sick, and summoned up a feeling that spread out from my body just enough to touch him. Wizards aren't all about blasting you with dark powers, it can be subtle too, just like with Grandma. A sense of urgency and forgetfulness permeated the air. This is the true art of dark magic—manipulating the energy you draw and actually making it into something subtle rather than just blasting away. It's a mental game, much more difficult to master but infinitely more useful.

The man became jittery and kept glancing at his watch. He drained the dregs of his mystery beverage then slammed the lid down on his laptop. He would be feeling like he had someplace to be, like he'd forgotten something important. He grabbed his coat and made a dash for the door.

I turned, winked at Kate and beamed. As she came over with our drinks I pulled a chair out for her. She sat, shaking her head.

"Aah, that's better."

"What's going on?" she accused, smiling in amusement but squinting at me. She knows me too well.

"Okay, I have an ulterior motive. I have to deal with Ankine Luisi now, and no, I'm not going to get you involved." A look of relief washed over her. "But I wanted to see you, and I, well, I wanted your opinion on her when you see her."

"So you woke me up, for the second time today, just so I could stare at women with you?"

"Hey, don't make it sound dirty. But, yeah. Not all women, just her. Tell me what you see when she comes along."

"And how do you know she will?" Kate took a sip of her overpriced, unpronounceable and calorie dense coffee, then sighed with pleasure. I drank my filter coffee and shrugged—I don't know what the fuss is about.

"Oh, she will. I've set some bait." I nodded at Oliver stood in the street, scowling at the people that passed, following some with his eyes as they entered or exited stores. He was looking for his next meal, sniffing out the lonely, the dispossessed, the alone or the weak, the ones that wouldn't be missed. I hope Kate never gets like that. I will do all I can to prevent it, and she's strong.

"How so?"

I turned from the window and let Kate have all my attention. She looked amazing. That inner fire that burned so bright after feeding is hard to resist, and I could see others in the place just as fascinated and drawn to her as I was.

To her credit, she didn't notice, or if she did she never acknowledged it. Classy through and through. "Because succubi are drawn to men, use them and abuse them, but they are also drawn to magic, like a faery to spaghetti. And blood magic is so close to what they know, what they are, that she'll be along to investigate. I'm sure of it. She comes shopping most days, apparently, so hopefully we can get a good look at her."

"And then what?"

"Then I at least know what she really looks like at the moment. It's not much to go on, but it's better than going in totally blind with no clue."

"What about us? She'll know we are here too, won't she?"

"She won't care about you, and she won't even care about poor Oliver there too much. But she won't be interested in me as I have no intention of letting her know I'm here."

"What, you gonna vanish or something?"

"No, I will shield myself. Here but not here, a part of the smell."

Kate sniffed the coffee-rich air, and looked at me, confused. "The smell?"

"I'm not just a pretty face. Look, I know I'm an enforcer, and some object to that, but I do good work, keep things together, on track, but I'm a wizard, Kate. I'm more than that."

"I know, Faz, but I still don't get the smell thing."

"I can blend back. You know how it is, that nobody in here sees me. They see a hot woman, but me? They see nothing. Succubi may be incredibly powerful, but they are fixated on men. Men they can take. Weak men, or men with a weakness. I will be nothing but a coffee-scented no-man. It's hard to explain, even to myself, but I can blend right back like you wouldn't believe. It doesn't work on all Hidden, but for Ankine Luisi it should. I will be the smell of this place. My magic will keep me hidden."

It's an old trick, just a blending really, but a different take on an old staple. One way out of many to be there but not there. A diverting of energy to make it easy to hide in plain sight. Subtle and yet immersive, the power of the mind, of the will, bending magic to make it do your bidding.

"Okay, if you're sure. But how long is this going to take? I'm tired, Faz. I need to rest, soon."

"Sorry, I should have never called. But I missed you."

"Haha, you've seen me loads today, more than for ages. Where have you been lately?"

I'd been keeping a low profile, trying to forget about her, keeping contact to a minimum as my feelings grew. It hadn't helped. It made things worse. "Just busy," I mumbled.

"Look, there she is."

We both turned to look out the steamy window. I let my ink vibrate as I sank into the ether, nothing but the smell of coffee and the slightest hint of a man. A technique that had come in handy over the years, perfect for Hidden that were so full of themselves they never searched for danger and believed themselves invincible.

Sickness enveloped me as I hunched forward and watched outside, but I remained little but a wisp of a man. A smell amongst unknowable beverages consumed all around me.

Even through the sickness I smiled as Oliver tugged at the collar of his t-shirt and looked ready to pounce on the nearest human as Ankine Luisi made her presence felt.

Damn, she was enchanting.

Stalking

As we watched the people go about their business, in and out of stores, buying clothes, food, pasties from Gregg's or the more expensive Cornish Pasty Pavilion, and blowing on the food in their mouth in that "Hot, hot, hot" way that's always comical as long as it's not you with burning meat on your tongue, I felt oddly relaxed considering I was stalking the most dangerous woman in the country. Maybe on the planet at that moment.

The Armenian swung her Debenhams bag in a carefree, what-a-lovely-day-it-is way, seemingly oblivious to the cooling afternoon and the dullness of the new paving already plastered with discarded chewing gum beneath her feet. She wore a light summer dress, striking yellow like a buttercup, sleeveless with a flared hem. A seventies original—I know my eras.

Her arms were slender, but nothing that would make you take a second look. In fact, she appeared entirely unmemorable. It was the dress that drew a little attention because of its simplicity and style, not the woman.

She had brown hair, rather straight, long but a little limp even though she held a plain umbrella to stop the rain. She was slim, verging on scrawny, with the body of a middle distance runner—not very curvy, but athletic and at the same time womanly.

Ankine Luisi's features were unremarkable. She was neither drop-dead gorgeous nor too plain, but somewhere in-between. Average, like most people are. You would look at her, then look away and go about your business.

As a succubus, the Armenian could take on any human form she wished. Even locked to our world, because of the time spent here, she could still manipulate reality in ways well beyond the abilities of most wizards or mages. Yet she chose, like she always had, a rather innocuous image. This was her true stroke of genius.

The truth is that men get nervous around extremely pretty women, or they simply think they have no chance and won't risk a rebuff, so you often find that truly exceptional looking females find it harder to get dates and attract male company than somewhat good looking ladies do. This is obviously why women seldom approach me. Haha.

Ankine Luisi thrived on men. Used them, spat them out, and moved on to the next, sometimes becoming involved in many at the same time. So she took on the form of someone that was entirely approachable, and was able to set her sights on unsuspecting males without doing anything to scare them off or make them reticent.

We are, and I hate to admit it—but after over a hundred years of being a man and seeing how we behave, I can't deny it—fickle, easily led astray, and suckers for anyone that actually takes a shine to us.

Watching Ankine Luisi go about her business in a carefree, happy-with-the-world way, was like a lesson in how to bend a man to your will. Kate and I watched, entranced.

There was a way about her. She walked with confidence, yet without being cocky or unapproachable. She had amazing posture, and smiled and acted around men in ways that made me feel ashamed to be born a member of such a weak gender. What was wrong with us? Why were we so pathetic?

She would "accidentally" bump into men, giggle and tilt her head just so, smile and hold eye contact a fraction longer than necessary. She touched arms, kept her hand there, slowly drew it away, and the results were amazing to watch. As she moved off, the men would turn and smile, lost in a daze of boosted confidence and wonder at the woman they had just met.

She would haunt their dreams. She would go to them and a sense of her would always remain. This was her power. That contact, that sexual chemistry, it took something from those men, gave her a tiny piece of them. The magic that is in all of us, some of it would be hers, making them that little bit more empty inside, less connected to the magical world.

It increased her essence, her power, her life-force. She became stronger, better able to be who she was. A succubus that could ensnare you and take advantage of your weakness because you are just a man and have no control over your urges or your need to be wanted and loved and made to feel special.

Women feel the same way, I know, but it's different. We are weaker, and in her presence even the strongest man would find it nigh on impossible to resist her. If a few seconds of her company made men forget where they were going, or what they were doing, then imagine what a few hours, or a night in her company would do to a man. They would be hers.

This was exactly what she had done to Mage Teppo Quimby, Ambassador of the Finnish Dark Council.

The man was a fool. But not as foolish as Oliver.

"What's she doing now?" Kate couldn't get closer to the glass if she tried, and I had to stop myself doing the same.

But I remained motionless, hidden, kind of put out if I'm honest that Kate even remembered I was there. Maybe that's the connection we have? I hope so.

We watched as Ankine Luisi finished with her flirting, and finally made it to Oliver. She'd known he was there, and was in no hurry, yet Oliver seemed entirely oblivious to her. He really was a fool. So caught up was he in his own sense of self-worth and invincibility that he forgot not everyone is just potential food.

She circled him, like a shark circles a drowning fisherman, smiling and twirling her black umbrella so rain spun off and drops caught him on the nose. He drew his attention away from an overweight man entering a bookstore and rubbed at his face with a frown. Then their eyes locked before she looked away, coy and flirtatious.

He actually licked his lips, like dinner had been served, still with no idea it was he that was on the menu. He forgot about me entirely, never even glanced at the coffee shop as he swaggered over to Ankine Luisi.

She cocked her head to the side and closed her umbrella as the rain gave up to regroup. It was a fascinating mating ritual, entirely one-sided.

The Armenian looked around, but seemed satisfied that nobody else was of more interest. She rubbed at her arm, from her wrist up to her shoulder, drawing Oliver's eyes to hers, entrancing him. With full lips hardly moving, she spoke. The already captivated vampire stepped closer, face flushed, lost in her.

This man would rip the throat out of a human being given half the chance, had killed countless, cared nothing for what he saw as weak creatures, but he was helpless. His blood magic worked against him as it drew the Armenian succubus to his power—more for her to consume—and he appeared unaware of what was happening.

He stepped closer at her words, but something changed and she turned, maybe looking at us, maybe at the building, but it was impossible to tell. She acted as though it was a little too easy. A vampire of his age and power so easily taken, and out in the open, in daylight no less. Or maybe she simply lost interest and had already grown bored.

As Oliver spoke, Ankine Luisi lifted a hand to her mouth, tittering like a schoolgirl. She nodded.

He inched forward and puckered excited, dry lips. She kissed him. Gently, lightly, and tenderly. He practically fell flat on his face.

With that she was gone. Skipping away, bags swinging in that carefree way of hers, presumably to continue her daily spending spree.

Oliver was bent double, hands resting on shaky, thin thighs. He remained that way for maybe a minute, getting odd looks from passersby, then he stood.

He was, to put it bluntly, seriously pissed off.

"Well, if she can do that to a vampire like Oliver, I am guessing there won't be much of your Ambassador left by now," said Kate, leaning back, the spell broken.

I let the magic fade, felt myself again, only minor sickness, and turned to her. "I think you're right, Kate. Well, what do you think?"

"I think you are in a lot of trouble, Faz Pound. I think that you better watch your step or she will eat you up and spit out the gristle you like to call muscle."

"What, me, get mesmerized by a woman of magical powers? As if?" I smiled at her, hoping she got the lame attempt at humor.

She did, so ignored it completely. "Just be careful. But I can't help you, Faz. She is an odd one, that's for sure. I've never seen anything like that. She's like a vampire when we, you know, sort of glamor people, only she's a real expert."

"Don't feel bad. It's what she does, and she's had a lot of practice." That was the bit I was worried about. Ankine Luisi was true Hidden, a creature wholly born of magic. I was a man who knew a bit of magic and got sick to the stomach if I tried to push the boundaries. Plus, in case you haven't noticed, I kind of act like an idiot around sexy ladies.

"Goodbye, Faz." Kate got up and kissed me for the second time that day. I put a hand to my cheek like I was in a bad movie. I watched as Kate walked out the door, ignored Oliver—who was still far from right—and was gone.

Oliver glared in at me. I guessed I'd better go visit Teppo Quimby before Ankine Luisi finished her shopping.

There was still an hour or more before the stores closed so I had plenty of time. I wanted to see what condition he was in, and if he could help, before I confronted her. Again. I wished more than anything I could remember what had happened the night before, but I had nothing.

Maybe it was a good thing. I assumed that whatever had happened wouldn't exactly bolster my confidence. Not only had a previous meeting with her ended with me killing an innocent man and the burden I now had to carry, but she'd also put me off chess, and I loved that game.

What was the best way to deal with her? Use as much magic as I possibly could to protect myself, don't look her in the eye, and suck as much of her magic out of her as I could before she wiped my mind and I killed another Grandmaster. Even that had more holes in it than an elf's ear, and the consequences for taking magic from a true Hidden meant it was a seriously bad idea. Still, it was better than nothing, and all I had.

Yeah, not much of a plan, but I'm a lover not a thinker. I hadn't done much of either lately, especially the loving bit.

I got up and drained my coffee. I should have ordered a stronger one, but I didn't know how to ask for it. The Mighty Scowler at Baristas, Ancient Dismisser of Complicated Coffees, left the building.

The end was approaching. I just hoped I managed to survive so I could ask Kate to come help me recuperate and I could bill Rikka for my suit and the bonus I was expecting for what was becoming one of the worst day's work I'd ever had. I hadn't even got to the main job yet, so, yeah, it was a very bad day.

Outside, I was lost in thought as I turned to go back to the car. Then I remembered Oliver. Damn, it was probably best to take him with me, just so Taavi knew I had dealt with the problem. Last thing I wanted was him on my back after the day I'd had already, and much as I loathed Oliver it was better than being summoned by Taavi and getting picked up by the Chinese goons again.

I turned, but he wasn't there. Well, his loss. No way would I go looking for him. I headed back to the multi-story car park, the aroma of coffee trailing behind me like memories of nervous conversations with confident baristas. The streets were slowly emptying of shoppers, the TV crews and the law had long since given up the morning incident as maybe bizarre but certainly not supernatural, and I, the invisible everyman, unassuming and entirely forgettable, pulled the parking ticket from my wallet as I got off the street and out of the rain.

"You set me up," growled Oliver, standing by the machine I had to use to pay so I could exit.

"And you let her glamor you. You're an old vampire and you let her glamor you. Don't you—" I was shoved from behind. Then I was off my feet and before I had a chance to say something clever at the smug sneer on Oliver's face I was up three flights of stairs and on the top level of the car park, back out in the rain, dumped on the wet ground with Oliver, and two other vampires stood in front of me, fangs showing, looking less than happy.

"You owe me for a new suit," I said as I got to my feet.

"You owe me more than that," said Oliver.

Three sets of fangs shone dully. Maybe it was time to think of a career change.

Unhappy Vampires

"Are you nuts?" I shouted as I stood and felt my tattoos whirl dark magic around my body in pulses of sickness that I knew had already turned my eyes as black as my anger, sparks of silver making the vampires shimmer and my body hum in tune with the Empty.

See, this is why these damn vampires are such a nightmare to be around. Most of them can't control themselves if they feel affronted. What's worse is that if they do get angry, and the plea for vengeance leaks into the communal vampire consciousness, then you can bet there will be a few more than keen to back them up. They love a bit of drama, and if that involves sucking on someone full of magic then all the better.

"You set me up." Oliver was livid. Worse, he had the hunger. His encounter with Ankine Luisi had pushed all his buttons and he craved sustenance. She'd geared him up then taken away a part of him. He needed to replace that lost energy and what better way than a snack of Spark?

"It was only to see who she was, what she was like. You know as well as I do that Rikka and Taavi want her gone. She can cause all kinds of trouble for everyone. Not just our Council, but yours too. Why do you think he told you to tag along?"

"I'll deal with her, and he'll thank me for it. But first we'll deal with you."

"Not such a hotshot now, are you, Spark," said the girl from that morning, the one in the tree. Her friend was next to her. He sneered, a poor attempt at copying Oliver. The younger vampire looked more like a bad imitation of Elvis than an evil immortal. At least Oliver had his lip curl down to perfection.

Both were still immature by vampire standards, maybe twenty or thirty years into their new life, and both seemingly only late twenties when it happened. They wore current fashion, which looked wrong on a vampire. Most are pretty sharp looking and have a sense of individuality, not these two—they had a lot to learn, if they lived. Suddenly, I understood what had been bugging me about them both since I met them that morning. They were trying too hard. Too hard to blend in, too hard to be badass, and they failed on all fronts.

"Look, kids," I said, holding my hands out to them even though that probably wasn't such a good idea. I leaked a little, and dark energy, with twisted faces and other warning effects I'd mastered long ago, sort of shot toward them and burned through the asphalt. They jumped back and Oliver growled. "Oops. Look, I've got no argument with you two, Oliver either if he just behaves. Do you know what kind of trouble you will be in when Taavi hears about this?"

They looked at each other then at Oliver. I saw the uncertainty. "Okay, best outcome is, you kill me, and Oliver defeats Ankine Luisi, the most powerful woman on the planet. The woman that just glamored him surrounded by a bunch of shoppers. Worst outcome is, I kick your asses and tell Taavi. Now, if you leave, then I'll say no more of it to anyone, and me and Oliver here can sort out our differences alone."

"We're not scared of you, Spark," said the young male, stepping forward. He brushed freshly cut hair behind an ear, the red locks stiff from some kind of product. I swear he did it thinking it made him seem relaxed and cool.

Kids, what are you gonna do? "Okay, last chance. Leave us to it, or else."

"Or else what?" he said, puffing out his chest, showing his fangs like it made a difference to me.

"Or else I will pull all that you are out of you. I will destroy you. I will take your magic, your blood magic, and I will send it back to the Empty and you will be your true age." I could see the uncertainty, the fear of what he would be without his blood magic. The girl too. She was thinking about it. How old were they? I wondered if they were older than I'd thought. Maybe sixty? Older? A far cry from the youthful bodies and looks they had now anyway. They were just a bit on the daft side, bless their cold, vicious hearts.

"Not if we win." Before he changed his mind he came at me, impossibly fast, and his hand was almost at my throat when I erupted into darkness.

Vampires think they have a handle on terror. Well, they don't. Wizards, mages, even necromancers, we and our kind know the true horror of what it is to work through magic. It defines us, it is us, and I am an enforcer. I channel it, I take it from you, I draw magic into myself and I do not let myself be intimidated.

I thought of myself in a bubble, a solid yet clear shield, impenetrable to magic or matter. He bounced off me like a ball hitting a wall and slammed into the ground, shocked and shamed. I felt the hurt of the magic use thunder through my veins and cloud my mind for a moment before it passed. A calm before the inescapable payback to come. Letting my anger and deeper emotions fuel me, I directed the Empty through sheer force of will, summoning knowledge and insight into the ways of magic and did what I do best. I sparkled black and silver as my years of training were unleashed.

A monstrous spout of pure, dark magic spasmed along my tattoos, down my left arm and out to his head with no subtlety whatsoever.

He was charred like a burn victim. Hair gone, features burned away, head steaming, blackened skin flaking as I drew my arm back to my side and with it his blood magic.

He fought back, using up bodily reserves to reverse the effect, and his usual features returned as his body visibly shrank with the effort—his torn and burned clothes hanging loose. But even as I and the others watched, he began to change again.

I sucked and took in a massive, deep breath, draining his magic, pulling it from him as his body convulsed and dark magic flashed from his withered frame like a reverse lightning strike, shooting into my mouth as I gulped it down like a hungry demon.

"Yum," I said, just to freak him out. It always works. "I'm the soul-eater. I will devour you whole and spit out the husk of your mind." Gotta have some drama, it makes the fight easier as they battle with the terror.

I was getting sicker by the second, and I'd made my point.

Using every ounce of willpower, never wanting to stop taking what was neither his nor mine, I slowed the flow, reversed my breathing, and gave a little back.

He looked truly terrible. Face wrinkled, skin a mess of blotches and blackened patches, but he took back a few years, gratefully.

It was enough. Killing him, or doing too much irreversible damage, would only cause trouble for me, Rikka, and the whole Dark Council.

I let him be.

The struggle not to fall over and cry at that moment was almost irresistible as the hurt was almost too much, but I let the magic flow out and away to where it belonged.

"Be... thankful... I... let you... live," I gasped, as I threw up foul black bile then stood tall, defiant.

With a body composed of nothing but pain and booze sickness times a thousand I stared down at the girl, who took one glance at the blackened, wrinkled old face of her friend and cringed like she'd been beaten as a child and didn't want to be hit again. I studied her, a moment of insight revealing what she really was, and why she put on the mask of insolence. Life is never simple, there's always something going on underneath that shapes us, a past that makes us who we are.

Understanding, I nodded. She grabbed her friend then was gone in a blur. I wondered how we looked if a Regular was spying on us. Our magic would mask us, so would we look like a bunch of drunks shouting incoherently at each other? Me flinging invisible punches, the magic only seen by us?

I turned to Oliver. "He'll live, but it will take him years to recover, if he ever does. And he will always be whatever age he truly is now. Your fault, Oliver, and Taavi will hear of it. Those kids will be squealing to your master right this minute. Ugh." I threw up again, but kept an eye on Oliver. I needn't have worried; he never moved a muscle.

My skin was on fire, my eyes felt like I'd been punched by a troll, repeatedly, and my emotions were gone, non-existent. No hate, no love, no sympathy. Nothing. The price of the magic.

It takes so much, gives back, too, but always at such a terrible price. Sometimes I just want to be left alone, go home, watch TV, and maybe do the garden, but I always come back for more.

This dark world of ours, it has its own special kind of power, and it isn't only the magic. It's the world, the people, the chance to be different. To walk in the shadows where humans challenge the very essence of life.

Yeah, I know, but we all have our flaws.

"Stay away from me, Oliver. Let me do my thing, and then go crawling back to your master and tell him I, not you, dealt with this problem. It's my job, and you better not stand in my way."

"Just like your parents. Always got to be the one in the right." Oliver flinched at his own words, then sneered like he always does. The final act of a coward. He was gone.

I stood on the top story of a car park, fizzing from the rain, little more than a black ghost, half gone to the unknowable world of the Empty, then sank to my knees once I knew I was alone. I still felt it, the taste of that vampire on my tongue, in my mind and my heart, and it left me a little more empty inside. Cold. Poor Kate. This was what she would become unless she fought it with every ounce of her body and mind.

What did he mean? Like my parents? Was it him? I couldn't think about that, not with so much to do, and so much hurt.

The taste of a vampire, of their soul, is a terrible thing. It's hard, uncaring, and empty of emotion for anything but their own kind. They love their own with a fierce intensity that is, in its way, beautiful and beyond compare. But it means there is nothing left for anything else.

They have contempt for humans. Vampires care nothing for the species they arose from. They are as cold as a deep pool at midnight, oblivious to what it once was to be human and feel things, good and bad. They are selfish and they are cruel, too. These creatures of blood magic enjoy the hurt and the pain they inflict.

I should have killed them all and stomped on their dessicated corpses, fed them to the zombies.

But I didn't.

I would be meeting Oliver again once I finished my job. If he had anything to do with me losing my parents then I would... I stopped the thought. I was dark and ugly enough inside already, if I let myself spiral deeper I would never surface again.

I cried instead.

Not for them, but for Kate, and for me, because I knew I would never give up on her. That was its own kind of selfish, for me and for her. Delaying the inevitable, maybe, fooling myself she would be different. Or was I just delusional?

Or maybe, just maybe, our friendship would be enough.

I hoped so.

I threw up, again, and I didn't have another clean suit.

"Hey, got any more Marmite?" came the baritone of Intus. "Oh!" He stared at me, looked around to discover where he was—I'm sure it was his bum, I think I recognized it, so couldn't think of it as anything but a he now—then his ears flattened as he hopped onto my outstretched arm, with my palms still down in a puddle. He—I like it as a he— stared up at me with concern. "Bad time?"

I nodded. "Bad day. Sometimes I think it's a bad life."

"Don't be daft, you got it made."

"Is that right?" I asked as I got to my knees and he hopped down, splashing in the puddle that came over his shins.

"Yeah, course it is. Nice house. Kate. Your Grandma. That thing you call a fridge, full of food. Friends, like me." He beamed, ears straight, then flat, not knowing which emotion was right. I couldn't help but chuckle. "See, you're sorted. And you can buy Marmite whenever you want."

"If you love it so much, why don't you, you know, just take it from stores or people's houses?"

Intus looked at me like I was an epic fool, and I guess I am. "Spark, of course I can get Marmite anywhere, and whenever I want. It's not about that. We're friends. I come to you because we are buddies. For help or to hang out. Or to help."

"Oh." Yes, I am a complete idiot most of the time. Oblivious to the things that should be cherished the most.

"Idiot."

"I've been getting that a lot today."

"I'll bet."

"Um, no Marmite on me, I'm afraid. But you had a whole jar."

"Um, yes, about that. We kind of made up, me and Illus."

"Yeah, I saw. Ugh."

"Oi, don't you judge me. Well, we made up, and, er, the kids have got a real taste for it."

"The kids! But it was only earlier that you..."

"And your point is?"

"How can you have kids already? It's only been a few hours."

Intus frowned at me, like he was rethinking our friendship. "Have you gone a bit funny in the head?"

I had to think for a moment. Maybe the vampires had won after all. "Um, no, I don't think so."

"You do know how we have babies, right?"

"The usual way?"

"I don't know what you mean by that, but you know I'm an imp?" I nodded. "So, we have had babies." I just stared at him. "I live in the true Hidden, so..." he prompted.

I shook my head. "Nope, I got nothing."

"So that's not this world, is it? Our time isn't yours, and imps don't really see your time anyway. It's rather odd."

"Um, okay."

"So, we have six," Intus said brightly. "And we're out of Marmite."

"Congratulations. On the kids, not being out of Marmite."

"Thanks."

"Er, Intus?"

"Yes?"

"You do know that I just fought off a load of vampires, right?"

He nodded. "I do. I was waiting until it was over with."

"Oh."

There was a bit of an awkward silence. Then we both burst out laughing.

"Well, just thought I'd check for Marmite. See you."

"Thanks, Intus, and congratulations again. You are a true friend and I will never forget that."

Intus looked at me, all serious for a moment. "Good."

He was gone.

It's easy to miss what's staring you in the face sometimes. Of course he didn't come to see me for Marmite. He came because he was my friend, and if he needed help he thought of me, and when he knew I needed help he came to cheer me up.

I picked up my parking ticket from the wet ground and wondered if it would still work in the machine. It's just one damn thing after another some days.

Fish and Chips

I sat on a damp wooden bench and let the grease seep through the paper, staining my suit trousers. It didn't matter, they were trashed anyway. Maybe I should start wearing jeans instead?

The piping hot food warmed my insides and took away the worst of the sickness. It soaked up the cold emptiness of vampire and eliminated the taste of the blood magic I loathed with every part of my being.

Why couldn't life always be this simple? Sitting on a bench, feeling full of cheap food, watching people dashing through town to get to the pub, picking up takeaway or doing a little last-minute shopping before the stores closed? I had no such luxury, and I ate fast, knowing I had to get to the Embassy, and soon. But I'd had to eat, there was no choice. I was drained, empty inside, and would be good for nothing otherwise. And besides, I like fish and chips.

Stuffing the last piece of crispy cod into my mouth, I scrunched up the paper and put it in the bin.

My lips felt wet, so I licked them, a strong taste of salt and vinegar my only reward. Then more salt. This time it was wet.

I was crying again. For me? For Kate? For them, the Regulars who knew nothing of this life? Maybe for all of it, for everyone. Probably mostly just for me.

What did Oliver mean about my parents? Had he known them? There were plenty of reasons why their paths would have crossed; our world is a small world.

Had he killed them or been involved in their deaths? I would find out. When they died, killed by vampires, their passing had torn a rift between Hidden that still rippled. Rikka had gone apoplectic, threatening to wipe out every last vampire unless Taavi found, and delivered, the culprit. Rikka called in every favor, every contact, every available human or true Hidden he could to find out what happened, but there was never a satisfactory conclusion and the killer, or killers, remained free. Alive.

Grandma had looked after me then, dealing with my craziness, my juvenile threats and promises of dark vengeance. It wasn't long before I ran, to the only man I thought could help. To Rikka.

Against my now dead parent's wishes, I immersed myself in the darkness and became what I am today. A man with a part missing, unable to look at another vampire without wondering, was it you?

It was mine and Grandma's first, and only, real fight. She may have been a remarkable witch then, but my parents had wanted something different for me, even though they were both from this world I suffer in.

They probably knew it was inevitable deep down, but they tried to keep me away, keep me a Regular. I jumped in headfirst after they were ripped from me, and I haven't surfaced for air yet.

I doubt I ever will.

Shaking memories of over a century ago, I walked over to the car, Rikka's car, and got in. I was on a side street, nearly at my destination, and it had only been ten minutes to order and eat.

The car hummed to life, but the new car smell did little to improve my mood. With a sigh, every part of me screaming for rest, for peace, I put my seatbelt on and pretended I wasn't as tired as an imp after making six babies in an afternoon.

Checking my mirror, I pulled out into the almost deserted gray roads of Cardiff. I looked at the people walking past, on their way to meet up with friends, or a date at the cinema, maybe for a meal. They seemed happy.

That's not my world though, for my sins. Visiting disgraced dark wizards and trying to deal with a powerful Armenian succubus, that's my world.

Strangely, I began to whistle.

I would not die that day.

I crossed my fingers, in case it helped.

Mr. Ambassador

The Finnish Dark Council Embassy reflects perfectly quite how seriously they take their magic.

Whereas other countries, if they have an Embassy in little 'ole UK at all, are usually based in London—as that's where the action is in terms of money, nightlife, and powerful Regulars—the Finns have their Embassy in Cardiff, much like the other serious worldwide players. They want to be in the thick of the magic scene, not where they can most easily influence humans to further their own bank accounts and world business empire—which is vast and more powerful than you would believe.

It's a shrewd move, and those that have no representative in the city that is the seat of power for all things magic related are looked on as fools by both dark wizards and vampires, the two dominant species when it comes to magic.

Yes, it's true that the vampires refuse to cow-tow to wizards, ignore the Dark Council and pretty much keep their own Houses and Councils private, yet they are just as serious about business as everyone else —probably more so. Even they answer the call of the Hidden Council, and are never above a little wining and dining of anyone if it means money and increased influence.

The Finnish set up long ago in a rather grand townhouse, no expense spared, meaning it was stuffed full of overpriced antiques from mismatched eras and a lot of arcane tat that any self-respecting wizard, or species born into magic, would know is just for show.

Still, they are the de-facto homeland of all things esoteric so nobody has ever said anything, and besides, it was kind of nice. The cluttered, yet immaculately clean interior made you feel like you were a part of something, certainly better than having to deal with magic related issues while a bunch of muscle-bound misfits grunted and flung sweaty towels at you.

It was still overcast and felt like dusk even though it would be light for hours, but at least the rain had stopped as I parked. The street was quiet, tree-lined and smart, the kind of place where everyone painted their railings each year without fail, the windows got washed weekly, and dog poop bags were very much in evidence. Lined with Georgian townhouses with expansive windows and high ceilings, the properties were totally out of my price range.

After a hundred years you would think I would have amassed a fortune, but I'm not really bothered about money. If I was so inclined, I could just walk into places and take what I wanted, but I have lived in the same house for so long I wouldn't think of moving, and I have enough to live comfortably. What more is there?

Walking up the steps to the Embassy, I felt exposed, and like I really should have a proper plan, but it's not how I operate. And besides, I couldn't think of one. I rang the bell, just to be polite, and while I stood there for five minutes waiting to be let in I admired the goblin head shaped door knocker. It wasn't there the last time I'd visited.

"Wot you lookin' at, freak," said the silver door knocker, with a scowl.

"Just wondering what you do on your off days," I replied with a smile.

"Eat humans for being cheeky."

I pushed a finger up its brass nose and wiggled it around.

"Oi. Gerroff."

Before I got into an argument with a piece of door furniture, I was saved by a troll in a butler's suit. It opened the door, completely blocking any view of the interior, and grunted. Having only waited a mere five minutes there was no doubt they must have replaced the previous troll employee with a speedy and clever one.

After the usual one-sided conversation, I was ushered in and we stood in the large hallway, even large enough for a troll to move about freely. I knew the troll would take a while before it spoke, it had been a busy few minutes for it already. The hallway was elegant, and suitably atmospheric. The Finns really went in for the magic theme so there were the mismatched antiques, a lot of lamps casting suitably deep shadows on the collection of artifacts on show, plus a few paintings I knew were magic-infused—the eyes really did follow you around.

"You wizard?" the troll asked.

"Yes, I am. I was sent by Mage Rikka, as I just said."

The troll scratched at a lumpy head, a loud noise like pebbles falling into a bucket the result. "No remember. But remember wizard wait in library. Ambassador Teppo cast spell, make remember. I get key."

It wandered off, still scratching the confused head. Weird.

A few minutes later the troll returned, unlocked the door to the library—I'd been there before, years ago —and with a gracious, and slow, wave of an arm the size of a small mountain I was invited to wait inside while it went off to see if Mage Teppo was available. I knew he would be—it isn't polite to ignore a visit from an enforcer of the home country's Head of Council.

What was with the spell though? Just so the troll would remember to let a wizard into the library?

While I waited, I took a little wander around the room, all old, red leather wingback chairs, thick rugs, wooden shelves lined with books, interesting items with suitably spooky accent lighting—the usual.

A nervousness tickled my mind, making me edgy and uncomfortable, like I was stood on a ghost and it would haunt me forever as payback for being so inconsiderate—I actually looked, just in case.

Something was seriously off, I just couldn't quite put my finger on it. No ghosts, no imps hiding ready to play a mean trick on me, no fae ready to attack me with razor sharp wings, no demons hiding under the rugs, or vampires peeking from behind the thick, already drawn drapes, but my tattoos were itching like crazy and my mind was less than clear, and not just because it had been a very long day.

Turning my attention to the books again, as my half-fried synapses tried to tell me something, I knew right away what the problem was. These weren't merely books for show, these were proper books, stuff that shouldn't be there, shouldn't be anywhere.

They practically screamed at me, the draw of the magic and information they contained was so strong.

We aren't big on books, any of the Hidden, as they are too easy to lose or get stolen or burned by accident, and for as long as I can remember everyone who has become involved in magic learns through a teacher, through trial and error and practice, perfecting their preferred art form through instruction and immersion in the Empty, hardly ever by burying their head in books. It's just not how we do things. Some information is too dangerous to risk it ever getting into the wrong hands.

What I found on the shelves made me shudder, and that was just the titles. Where the hell had he got them from? Did he even know what they were?—of course he did. Was he completely insane?—my guess was, yes. Some of the books were worth more than a country. Titles I'd heard whispered over the years, myth and legend, never seen. The knowledge contained so important, so powerful, that in the wrong hands it would blow our world wide open.

Forget my little "accident" of the morning, this was the real deal. The real way to expose us all. There would be no going back once such information got out.

The dark shelves were rammed full of arcane tomes I knew right away were immensely valuable as well as powerful. You could do anything with a collection like this. You could rule the Hidden and Regular world. You'd pay the ultimate price though—I could feel the madness seeping through my pores just being in the room with them. This was too much, this was insanity on a shelf.

As I pulled out title after title, I began to feel sick, as the promise of what they contained, and the way they leaked, was enough to make me almost lose control because of the magic I was exposed to.

Such things should never be written, certainly not be left in the Regular world. That's not how we do things. Yet here it all was, books I never knew existed, books I had assumed were long gone, some mere rumors, now here, on the shelves. And I'd been invited in and allowed to see them.

It was time to go. Teppo had wanted a wizard to see, and that meant he was trapped. He wanted us to know, so we could do something. No way was I getting out alive if I'd seen this and Ankine Luisi found out.

Wasting no time, I headed to the door, wanting to grab as many books as I could but knowing it was fruitless, and which ones anyway? It opened before I was halfway across the room and the troll-cum-butler turned sideways, ducked, and stepped into the room.

"You stay."

"Can't. I just remembered I have an appointment. Say sorry to the Ambassador, but I will call again."

"No. Stay." The troll put out a hand, as if I could move past it otherwise—it was wider than the door and a lot taller. A hand went to its head again and it thumped it hard, as if trying to remove something. I swear it actually frowned. Then it said, "Wizard do thing to head. Mistress say not let people in library. Now you in. Must stay."

This was bad.

Fight with a Mountain

Teppo had tried to get a warning out, but Ankine Luisi had extended her influence to the troll, which was unheard of. The books, it must have been the books. She was beyond a mere succubus. She was learning other skills, knowledge not meant to be hers. "Look, buddy, I don't want any trouble, but if you don't get out of my way..."

The sickness rose as my tattoos sprang to life, stabbing and tearing at my flesh like a thousand fish hooks in their haste to activate. My eyes turned from regular vision to black, with the familiar specks most wizards seem to end up getting when in the magic zone. Normal sight faded and the magical world snapped into focus like putting on a pair of mystical glasses. It's a weird world, this Hidden world. So much to see; so many layers.

Magic shone at me from all directions. The books were alive with Hidden secrets, practically bursting their bindings.

The troll stood out like a beacon of pure magic. Timeless, and as ancient as the world itself. A creature born of fire and heat and unknowable pressures as it was spat out into the world at the beginning, amid the rock and chaos. I could see pockets of pink crystals, layers of various rock types, all hard as granite, and the jewel-like striations of red minerals that sliced through its massive frame. Even fragments of diamond that glittered in the light like a dangerous Christmas tree.

As the books practically came alive with my presence, screaming to be opened, to be put to use, the troll took a step forward, and I could read it easily. I was an intruder, a thief, not to be trusted and never allowed to leave. It was the guardian of the room and I was the enemy. The poor thing was tainted, corrupted by whatever the Armenian had learned, then practiced on the creature.

There was no choice, it was the troll or me. And I like me.

Stepping back, almost tripping over a strange stuffed cat, then edging around a low table like it would make a difference, I put all my focus on the troll, looking with Hidden-entrenched eyes at the structure of the creature. I could feel the dense pockets of rock, ageless and as impenetrable as the center of the earth.

My eyes searched the patchwork of minerals in its construction. Layer upon layer of compressed rock containing the history of the world, stretching back to the beginning, enduring and everlasting through the ages. I noted the flashes of thought as they slowly traveled around the priceless quartz brain, the simple structure of the body, the minimal nerves that offered little more than a faint reassurance as it moved but never felt, certainly not any pain.

I vibrated, thrumming faster and faster, going deeper and getting sicker and sicker, searching for weak spots.

And I found one.

Right beneath the left arm was a chunk of brittle slate, and I pushed out my hands, channeled everything I could through my tattoos and my body, sucking magic from the Empty like a landed fish gasping for oxygen as I let magic build and build inside myself until it erupted from my hands in all its dark, freakish, close to unmanageable, silver-specked glory.

The force hit the troll hard and it stumbled backward against a priceless Balinese carving that splintered into kindling. It said nothing, merely grunted as it recovered its balance and moved toward me.

It was angry, but you wouldn't know it. The heavy features were as blank as always. Again, I attacked the weak spot, summoning up magic that jeopardized my sanity and threatened to rip me apart as the intensity almost overwhelmed me, warning that soon it would leave me, and I would be a spent man, throwing up on the expensive rugs and a gibbering wreck for days.

Trolls are magic beings. Timeless. Pure magic. You never try to defeat them, you run. But I'm an idiot, and I couldn't get out the door, so rather than use magic to blast a window or a wall, I panicked and attacked what amounted to a boulder, but with fists. I was seriously regretting it.

The movable mountain took a step forward, and I pushed hard with all I had, air alive with the cries of demons and the damned that always clamored around a fracture in our world looking for a way through, a way out of their eternal torment.

Dark magic spewed from my mouth, my aching eyes and my hands tortured and raw with black pain, thick gobbets of manipulated Empty as concentrated as the primordial soup single-celled organisms once found themselves battling for survival in, to emerge into an uncaring world. I screamed as I broke through the boundaries of my limitations and the power became thick and with substance, became truth and power. Indefensible.

The troll stopped, slowly lifted an arm, and we both watched, mesmerized, as a piece fell off and clattered to the floor. Then another, and another, fracture lines cracking and spitting, steaming and popping like magma. Silence. A frozen statue of timelessness as it turned to nothing but inanimate rock as the energy lines that ran through its body returned to lifeless crystals and minerals.

An arm fell loudly to the floor, then another. Then large chunks rained down like a statue of ancient man overthrown by angry rebels, and tiny pebbles clattered down onto the growing mound of destruction, rolling away across thick rugs as lump by lump the proud creature, corrupted by an out of control true Hidden, broke apart, no longer the stoic member of an age-old race, now just my anger and my instinct to survive.

My magic use wasn't subtle, wasn't used to allow me to hide or shrink into the walls or become the air itself, it wouldn't work that way against a truly magical creature. I had to rely on something born of its own kind—brute force. Plus a little luck.

Soon there was nothing but a settling mound of rock. I watched as it turned to dust, then threw up.

My eyes bled black pain and silver tears, and my head felt as flat as a troll's sense of humor. Like my brain had been spread out thin and then all scooped up, neural pathways rearranged in no particular order.

I had to leave, so I crawled over the dust and shards of the troll, bits sticking to my greasy and magic-infused clothes. My hands were like claws, covered in sweat, veins popping, swollen and dark from the magic. Dust got up my nose, making me sneeze, but I kept going, knew I had to leave and warn Rikka. Warn anyone.

The air cleared a little as dust settled and magic receded. I scrambled over the last of the fractured troll, hands clutching wildly for purchase, getting nothing but sicker and then I was past, at the doorway.

Pushing on, not accepting it was over but wishing with all my heart it was, I recovered enough to get to my feet, fighting sickness, ordering it to wait, for this was far from over.

I wobbled, but remained upright. Gripped the door jamb, breathed deeply for a moment but coughed up something too nasty to look at, then pushed away with seized hands and muscles as tight as Kate's panties. I smiled to myself, knowing I wasn't totally lost, as a vision of her firm buttocks wrapped in pink underwear, cheeks wobbling like heavenly clouds, snapped me back to reality, gave me energy, meaning, a reason to go on. I felt strange, wondered why a perfect bottom would bolster me, but it was her, Kate, not just the bottom—although it is nice.

I staggered toward the front door, feeling like a robot in dire need of a tune-up, maybe a few new parts.

"Spark, what's going on?"

I turned to see Teppo Quimby coming down the wide stairs, gait awkward, clutching the banister like he would fall if he let go.

"You look worse than I feel," I said. He hardly looked alive at all. His face was ashen, cheeks terribly sunken. His hair was falling out in clumps, he couldn't stand upright properly, and there was so little flesh left on him that I was amazed he wasn't gnawing his own arm he must have been so hungry. An expensive suit hung off him like it was slung over a cross made of brittle sticks.

"Have you come to visit? How nice."

"Um, no, I was just leaving. See ya." I turned to the door. It opened.

Stood facing me, smiling and with her head angled quizzically to the side, was Ankine Luisi, complete with her days shopping.

"Hello," came a voice more beautiful than any sound I have ever heard in my entire life. "Won't you join us for a drink?" She glanced at Teppo on the stairs, then dismissed him.

The door closed behind her, although I didn't see her do it, or even notice as she moved into the hallway and I took a few steps back to maintain some distance.

"That would be... nice." I felt the sickness replaced with numbness, then a warmth that crept up from my crotch. My veins felt like liquid honey, sweet and delicious.

She smiled again, more charming than an angel, but as she took in the destruction at the entrance to the library there was a flash of anger before the divine creature turned her attention, her love, back to me.

My mind began to empty, all thoughts drifting away. Fluffy clouds, meaningless. I wanted her to own me, to be with this perfect creature for eternity. Nothing else mattered.

This was what I wanted, what I'd been searching for my entire pathetic life.

She would love me. She would care for me. She would soothe me when I cried in the dark.

She was an angel and I would be the luckiest man on earth.

I smiled. She smiled back.

Those eyes. Those pale, infinite green eyes.
I was in love. I was loved right back.
I was lost.
Almost.

Meeting the Armenian

Her eyes were beyond deep and beautiful, they offered the world. All there was. Pure beyond compare and what every man searched for, longed for, ached for and wept over. This was the answer to everything.

Every lonely hour, every desperate act of need, every foolish comment and action, every misdeed and dark thought, all was forgiven. All would be made better if she became the only one I loved.

I looked into her eyes, and fought.

Something changed as she saw the battle rage inside me, and anger rose. Real anger, deep and terrible, as infinite as her kind, and utterly without mercy.

Dark magic reared up once more, my body still thrumming like a well-tuned guitar, every muscle, every fiber of my being taut and primed even though the sickness was unbearable as the honey turned sour and the sugar turned to acrid bile.

My body battled against the deception the only way it knew how. It let the sickness and the magic turn the nectar to poison. Now I was truly lost, despondent and alone—she was the only one that could save me.

I refused anyway. Better to be nothing than to be hers.

My manly resolve vanished for a moment, and I felt my body and mind collapse as all around me turned dark and terrible—a warning, her punishment if I refused to accept her gracious offer.

My humanity, something I hadn't even realized I was close to losing, saved me. I thought of Kate and how she would be alone. And of Grandma and how she needed me to watch over her as she was to go on a date with a mortuary technician seer. I thought of Intus and of Rikka, and even Dancer. How was his nub of a finger?

"No," I managed to moan.

"No? You do not say no to Ankine Luisi. Nobody says no to the Armenian." She reached for me with pale and slender fingers as delicate and pure as a sprite's spirit, so beautiful my heart ached and everything in the world felt ugly in comparison. And I rejected it.

With my hands still locked up as claws, I batted her away, felt the impossible surge of hunger, longing, lust and passion pass between us. Promises of wild abandon and naked delights no Regular man could refuse. But the dark magic took over and I was so sick, so deep into the Hidden world, that her lies, her deception, her perversion of all that was pure and right in the world hit me like a flash of my own lost humanity.

I forced my mind to prise open my bent fingers, the severe cramp tearing at flesh and ligaments as the grip loosened, and I stared my fate in the eye defiantly as the angel's face twisted and spasmed, revealing a truth that would cause more innocent men to lose their minds.

Knowing I was almost lost forever, and with nothing to lose, I slammed my half open palm hard against my open mouth with such force my head whipped back. Locked fingers as hard as a troll's punch gouged deep lines across my cheeks and nose, and a tooth cracked as I took in the handful of troll dust still trapped in my contorted hand.

I swallowed.

To say it was dry would be like saying I was happy to become Ankine Luisi's next lover.

The succubus took a step back, confused, horrified, and afraid. Her beauty was gone. She was a plain woman in a nice yellow dress as I felt the dust burn my insides like the fires of hell.

"Oi, you can't do that. Are you off your rocker?" The faery scowled at me, magical motes of dust gleaming silver and gold all around her as she pinged into existence and wagged a finger right in my ripped and bleeding face.

"I know," I said, seriously in need of water. I felt the troll dust sink down my throat like the rock it was, and felt troll essence, ancient and immutable, battle against my ordinary self, changing me.

This was pure Hidden magic I'd consumed. A crime, an unjustifiable act that was always punished. What I did was taboo. A Law, inviolate, and it hardened me. Not my body, or my mind, but my emotions, turning me into not quite troll, not quite human.

"What do you think you are—"

The faery stopped Ankine Luisi with a whispery wave of her tiny hand, Ankine's words frozen as the faery turned back to me crossly, arms folded across her tight green dress and an ample cleavage. "Did you just eat a troll? You did, didn't you? I can see it on your lips, you foul man. Ugh, why are you all so horrid?" She tutted, an actual tut, and pointed at Ankine Luisi. "And what is *that* doing here? You know succubi are dangerous. Who let it loose? Who let it stay? It isn't supposed to be here."

I remained silent, unsure if she'd finished her tirade or not, not knowing if I could utter a word anyway. One thing you do not do, ever, is interrupt a faery. They are short to temper, not often keen on humans, take their work extremely seriously, beautiful, curvaceous, sexy as hell—in a strictly hands-off kind of way—and utterly cold and ruthless in their punishment. Their wings hurt too—they can rip a man's face to shreds faster than you can say, "Where's my skin gone? And why is my chin on the floor?"

"Excuse me? Do you think you could speak a little quieter? It's giving me a headache." Teppo was sat on the stairs, looking worse than a decades-old zombie without formaldehyde. I was amazed he could speak at all.

"Who's the corpse?" asked the faery, nodding in his direction. Beautiful, long and wavy blond hair sprinkled magic dust a wizard would sell his soul to bottle as she moved her adorable head. I struggled to stop obsessing over her ears—how could an earlobe be so perfect? I wanted to nibble it and lick it. Fae really do bring out mixed emotions in a guy.

"Victim." I managed to say through gritty aftertaste of troll.

"Right," said the faery, nodding.

Something was familiar about her, but I was loath to say anything, just in case I was wrong. The troll dust was gaining momentum, stopping me from feeling much, from caring. That would have been great if it was just me and Ankine Luisi, but it meant I could easily say the wrong thing in front of the faery and then it would be goodbye, Black Spark, hello, Dead Spark.

"Would you mind, now that you're here?" I pointed at my throat. The dust was coalescing, forming a hard lump as the troll essence fought to become part of the whole again.

I felt myself fade, harden like the rock inside of me, emotions stripped away, taking me to a cold place. To become troll. Abomination.

"Sure, no problem," she said brightly. A tiny sword appeared in her hand and she drew her arm back with an expert swing, ready to slice my throat.

"Whoa! No, I meant, get the dust out!"

"Oh, right. Oops." The sword vanished and she did a little spinning action with her hand, the air sparkling, sending shivers up and down my spine like the caress of a lover in the middle of the night.

My chest felt like my ribs were being ratcheted open and I couldn't breathe. I gasped for air and I'm sure my head ballooned to twice its normal size. I was a cannon, and a heavy troll cannonball was forcing its way up through a constricted esophagus way too small for such a dedicated lump of immortal rock.

A cough built and built, my throat felt like it would rip apart, and my whole neck extended grossly. I gasped for air as my obscene ingestion, a ball the size of an apple, exploded out of my wide-open mouth, arced high above my head, almost hitting the faery, then dropped to the carpet with a dull thud.

The black ball began to roll toward the already solidifying pile of dust and rock, but I put my foot on it, hoping it would give me some time. The troll would be back to being whole soon enough—no harm done to it. One thing I knew for sure though—I didn't want to be around when it came to its, albeit limited, senses.

I felt better instantly. "Thanks."

"Pleasure. Now, about your punishment."

The Truth About Fae

"Punishment, come on," I croaked and whined like a baby. "I only ate the troll dust so you'd come. I knew it was the only way out the moment I realized what the succubus had made Teppo do."

"What's a Teppo. Is it food?" She looked around with tiny wide eyes the color of love.

Fae adore food, they can't get enough of the human kind. The only problem is they find it hard to get to our world unless there is a serious magical disruption and they come to sort it out. "No, it's him, the guy on the stairs. The succubus has him and he's pretty far gone."

"Not really worth bothering with then, is he? Shall I, you know?" The sword appeared again and she swished back and forth with some practice swings, almost slicing the nose off Ankine Luisi.

"No, no, no. I want to make him better. Look at him, she's practically drained him of everything. He's a shell."

"Not my problem, is it? I don't mess about with stuff like that, I just make sure nothing happens that's against the Law. And you broke the rules." She stared at me sternly, the sword gone, replaced with a tiny finger waggling in front of my face.

I caught a glimpse of earlobe again and gulped. Man, those ears! "I said I was sorry." I was whining, and I knew it, but you really don't want to get on the wrong side of a faery.

Of all the magical creatures there are, and all the things that can happen to you by being involved in the Empty, fae are the most terrifying by far. Forget Ankine Luisi, forget vampires and all the rest, fae are what terrify most of us.

They are truly magical, the essence of magic, in fact. Immortal, impossible to understand, and utterly without remorse or forgiveness when it comes to breaking the Law. There are certain things you don't do, unwritten laws that our kind must all abide by no matter who we are or how powerful we think we may be.

You can be thousands of years old but to a faery that's a blink of a tiny, perfect eye. They have seen it all, know it all, and have made it their duty to ensure that the world of magic exists forever. Which means they enforce the Law that allows it all to continue. And one of those Laws is that you do not, ever, take on the essence of another magical and pure creature. Which is what trolls are, and which is what I had just done out of desperation.

"Sorry, sorry, sorry. It's all I ever hear. You humans are the worst. Always interfering, always messing up. I wish you'd never got access to the Empty. It's not yours, it's ours." She thumped her chest. It jiggled. I gulped and tried not to stare. "Magic belongs to magic creatures, not humans." Fae also like to rant. They have schools for it, and they take their lessons seriously.

"Hey, it's not our fault. We found it and it's part of us now. You know as well as I do that every human has magic inside of them. And if that—"

"That doesn't mean you are magical, it just means you have it inside, to make you alive at all. It doesn't mean you can go around eating trolls and asking me to kill succubus, or heal fools that let themselves get glamored. You lot are so needy."

"He doesn't exactly just look glamored, he looks like a skeleton. She's sucked the life out of him." I pointed at poor Teppo, still sat on the stairs, mostly oblivious, watching from behind a screen of incomprehension. He was fading, and fast. With Ankine Luisi still frozen and out of action I guess he wasn't linked to her and the full force of her draining of his essence was now in effect.

"That's his problem. His fault." The faery flew over to him and flitted about his bowed head, circling him faster and faster, then was back by my face in a flash.

I glanced at Ankine Luisi nervously, wondering if the spell on her would last. Then at the troll now halfway back to being what it was. Already the legs were complete, and as I watched, the dust moved faster, floating up and layering itself across the midsection, building the troll back to whole once more.

It would not be happy when it regained sentience and movement.

"Don't worry about her. She won't seduce you unless I let her loose. So weak, you lot. Especially you men. Only one thing on your mind." I'm sure she stuck her chest out and stroked her ear on purpose. She gave me a sly look, a hint of a wink.

"What about the victim?"

"I looked into his mind. You didn't tell me he's a wizard," she accused.

"You didn't ask."

"Don't you be cheeky to me or I'll turn you into something nasty. And as for him, well, it's tough. He should have known better, and besides, it's not my place to interfere with the natural ways of things."

"Wait, you can't leave him like that. She took him over, drained him, and she's been using him, collecting books. Books I never even knew existed. Books nobody should have, especially not a succubus."

"Like I said. Tough. Books are stupid, and humans are stupid. She's a succubus, what did you expect her to do?"

"Can I kill her, then? While she's like this?" I was feeling great, too great. Fae take away all the hurt, the pain, the sickening after-effects of magic use, but the comedown is brutal—I'm still not sure which is worse.

"Are you off your rocker!" The faery got real close, right up to my eye. Magic dust scatted and fell onto my nose.

I tried not to peek down her dress, and had to grab my own hand to stop myself tickling her ear. She almost poked me in the eye, and I felt real nervous about those wings so close to my only way of seeing.

"You so much as touch her now and I will send you to hell, the nasty one."

"Okay, okay, fine. But you have to do something. If you let her loose she's just going to go crazy." I had a thought. And there was nothing to lose. "You know that she's broken the Law, don't you?"

"How?"

"She's staying in the material world. She hasn't left for years. She's not just coming and going, she's permanent. That's not allowed, is it? Not for a succubus?"

"No, it is not. I shall have to have words with this one. But later, I've got other things to do. Be seeing you."

"Wait!" It was no use, she was gone. Damn fae, they are so full of themselves. They think they know best and they always stick to the rules. It's infuriating. Was this my punishment? To remain and be stomped to goo by semi-sentient rock? Or was that wishful thinking?

The troll almost had a head now. The last of the dust was floating up and moving fast, rebuilding the rock creature line by atomic line. It was like a printer except it was spewing out a troll, a soon to be very angry troll.

The air cracked and I smiled.

I'd forgotten I was in love. In love with the most beautiful creature in the world. What was I doing? Where was I? Somehow it didn't matter now.

I turned and stared into the eyes of Ankine Luisi, the most adorable female in the history of humanity.

She whispered, "Come," and held out her hand for me as she smiled with all the grace of a cloud of angels.

I put my hand out.

I'd do anything to touch those perfect fingers, be hers.

Forever.

You Again

I was lost, mesmerized and in love. More than love—I was completely and utterly helpless. This woman, this creature, was all that mattered. She looked into my eyes and I knew that my future was with her. She was the world, all there was. Perfect, and she had chosen me.

As I melted into her eyes, I knew I would do anything for her. Anything.

But as I moved my hand out to take hers, knowing it would mean I was hers forever, perpetual bliss, there was something else too, forcing its way through the fog of pure worship for this divine creature, banging at my mind like a troll knocking on a door. I tasted grit on my tongue, and swallowed it. A few grains of troll.

Something unlocked in my awareness, freeing me, as a tiny part of me hardened, burying emotion, leaving me detached. The Hidden magic of an always stoic creature making me a millionth part troll, enough to allow something through. I watched myself as if from a distance as my heart cooled, sweeping away my immersion and worship upon the altar of this beautiful creature I was about to surrender myself to so willingly.

"Come, be with me," the succubus said, making promises ever more inviting. So real I could taste the salt of her tears, the strawberry lips, feel the firmness of her skin, the welcome invite of her naked flesh that she would offer to me always, mine for the taking.

I swallowed, the dust particles falling deeper inside of me, another box of emotion locked away, pleasures of the flesh no longer all-encompassing.

Memories flooded in of the night before. They hit me all at once, selected scenes all overlaid one on top of the other in rapid succession like cards slapped down on cold marble.

Strobing lights of a nightclub, me tugging on Teppo's arm as thin as a child's, skin hanging loose, devouring himself from the inside.

Him turning. Me seeing that the man was already lost. Eyes haunted, flesh eaten away as the fire of lust and obsession burned ever brighter, obfuscating everything else from his mind. Me shrugging, knowing I had to leave before it was my turn.

Being handed a drink by Ankine Luisi. Me turning away, not looking. The music pounding through my body.

Lights blinking and confusing me as I tried to drag Teppo away while Ankine runs to the dance floor, flinging herself about. Uncaring, knowing, yet wild and with utter abandon.

The music getting louder, men crowding around her, everyone dancing to her rhythm, the wildness contagious, the whole club caught up in her charm.

Faster and faster, her a whirling dervish. Ankine Luisi, the infamous Armenian, spinning in a circle. Men stomping their feet, pounding on the floor with bloodied hands. Women transfixed, confused. Men adoring.

Teppo screaming for help, eyes haunted, lost but back for a moment. Me dragging him across the dance floor, to get us away. The music off the scale. Faster. Louder. Lights strobing as insanely as the crowd. The walls vibrating, closing in.

Men grabbing us, me brushing them off. Ankine Luisi going wild. My tattoos pulsing to the music, to the beat, me trying to summon up the Empty, draw it into me, blast them all out of the way and her too. Send every last one of them to hell, uncaring of the consequences or who might see, knowing she has to be stopped and for good.

My ears crawling with music, my body moving to the rhythm, the magic not coming at me right. Not enough there for me, all taken by her. Spinning around us all, caught up in the madness, the love, the worship of the most beautiful creature there has ever been.

I was jumping, dancing with Teppo, with the men and the women. Her at the center, us worshiping.

Her eyes closed in pleasure, us around her in a circle, pointing at her, calling for her attention.

Then me and her. Me swinging her in a circle faster and faster, her head back, laughing.

Then the sickness.

Somehow, I let her go, and she fell against the crowd, and I double over, my ink saving me from being lost forever. The sickness snapping me back to semi-reality and I ran, crouched over, body screaming in agony and shame as the Empty poured into me and dragged me away.

Now out in the dark streets. The rain fizzing off me but I don't even notice. Clutching at my stomach, revelers emptying from the clubs, laughing and joking, me just another casualty of drink and debauchery.

Lost, I wander, not knowing who I am or where I am, knowing I just have to get away from the city center, from the music. From her.

Cats watch from the dark, foxes patter past me in silence, car headlights blinding me as I stumble across roads lit by streetlights and empty office buildings.

Then people. More traffic. A desperate dawn clawing away the night, revealing damp grass and a chance of salvation.

And then the park. I stumble to a seat, sit and stare at the chess pieces. I hear the man's voice. "Your move."

I see the game, know it is mine. The magic still in me, not sent away as it should have been. The curse of the succubi trying to call me. I make my moves and I say, "Checkmate."

He gets angry and I get even angrier. I hate what I am, and I don't want to live like that, so I blast the magic out, to purge myself and be me again, but I direct it at the Grandmaster. I don't know what I'm doing. I am lost, and then I know, know enough to flee. I'm running. I'm away. I'm me again.

I snap back to reality, and my fingers are inches from Ankine Luisi's. This time she will never let me go. I'll be another one of her victims. I won't let that happen.

She is so beautiful, impossibly so. Teppo moans behind me, as if realizing she has already forgotten him, and he will be left without her love and attention.

The troll is almost complete now, dust spinning around the half-head, dropping into place, filling in the gaps, the whole massive body surrounded by tiny particles that slot and snap into place, soon to make the Hidden creature whole. Already, fingers are slowly twitching and legs begin to move. It will be over soon. So will I.

I urge, forcing the magic to flow. My tattoos jump to life, making me sick and I love it. Welcome the pain and the humiliation as it makes me human. There is acceptance—I know I am weak, and frail, a mere man, but I will not be beaten. I will not be taken.

It builds, circles within circles within circles, erupting out of my body, me summoning the Empty even as it overwhelms me. But the power allows me to focus, and I bend and pick up the rock that almost escapes as it moves back to the troll to complete it. My still-spasmed, half-clawed hand clutches it tighter than a faery's grip on a meatball, and while my other is still reaching for Ankine Luisi as I stand again, I see our fingertips are a hair's breadth away from each other.

Soon I will be lost. Soon I will be hers.

She smiles. She knows. She laughs.

The magic comes in wave after wave and I do the impossible. I close my hand and the ball of magic that is part of a timeless creature is crushed, turned to dust.

My smile feels good, and I spit out what remains of the troll inside of me and add it to the pile in my hand. I say something stupid like, "No thank you, I prefer blondes," and I shove the dust between her gorgeous, heavenly lips, and I can see the moist tip of her pink tongue that promises so much I ache to my bones.

Then it's covered in dust and I blast her mouth with all I have left inside of me and she jumps back and swallows.

The troll bellows behind me, and I turn as the doorway and wall tear like paper as the monstrous magical being walks straight through the too small opening and heads directly for Ankine Luisi.

"You eat troll. Break Law." It thunders toward us, huge legs eating up the distance in three paces. The focused troll shoves me aside like a doll, and a thick arm thrusts out faster than I have ever seen such a creature move in my life.

It grabs Ankine Luisi and pulls.

Her throat is ripped out and the troll flings away flesh then reaches back, grabs her windpipe and yanks on it, tearing it right from her body. With surprisingly dexterous fingers, it tears open the windpipe like it's removing cheap wrapping paper and pulls out the hard lump that is itself.

The troll puts the lump on top of its own head and it is complete. We both stand there, immobile, as Ankine Luisi claws desperately at her tattered neck.

She shimmers and leaks Hidden magic as the world vanishes, becomes original pain and blinding darkness, strobing silver and terrible light like the corrupted nightclub. We watch, the troll impassive, me little more than sickness, as her body morphs.

She is the woman I see before me, then she is blond and curvaceous, then she is dark-skinned and slender, then she is short and then tall, now brunette and wearing a costume from ancient history, and she is every woman from every continent, and she is every woman from every time, her shape and clothes shifting one to the other over and over.

The world empties, sucked down a drain like fetid, lumpy magic, and then she is who she really is. A demon. Her face pure hatred for humanity and for men. She snaps. Her body is a ghost, darkness and light, beautiful and terrifying. Her tail whips at the door, and her clawed hands reach for me while leathery wings beat against the wall and the high ceiling. Her body is perverse.

The air in-between us is scattered with sparkling dust and the faery appears once more. I catch a hint of earlobe and the sickness displaces. "You broke the—" she begins to say, then realizes she is where she was moments ago.

"I knew I recognized you from somewhere," the faery says. "You're Spark. Black Spark."

I don't know how she knows me, and I look at her ear one last time as the succubus reaches for me and I know the faery is too late and I have failed. "Huh," is all I manage. My last words and all I say is, "Huh." What a way to go.

"Yes, you saved a friend from that stupid elf, must be a while ago now."

"I... what?"

She nods at me, and I remember long ago when I saved a faery, thinking that doing such a favor could never be a bad thing. She smiles at me and winks, and she hums and sings, twirls a finger and Ankine Luisi is gone.

"Put her back where she belongs. In men's dreams. For now."

The faery flutters in front of us, spreading magic dust everywhere, then looks around, presumably for food. I want to lick my finger and dip it in the beautiful faery sprinkles, but I know now is not the time. The troll is scratching its head. Teppo is still on the stairs, head in his bony hands.

He's crying. I am too.

I sink to the floor, just lie there as I feel sicker than I have ever felt in my life, and it has nothing to do with the Empty. Not caring about anything, I curl up into a ball and wish that Grandma was there to make me a cup of tea.

I think of Kate, then oblivion comes and I am free of this world.

Just for a while.

Time to Wake Up

Maybe I lay on the dust-scarred carpet for eternity, maybe seconds. Either way, I was defective, incurable. Ill like I have never felt in my life as unwelcome reality pushed back in. It infiltrated my black heart with an insistent buzzing—like a dragonfly's wings scratching at my dreams of emptiness.

This was no dragonfly though, this was a faery. I opened an eye reluctantly, worried about what I would see. The faery was sat on my nose, peering at me like I was some kind of specimen in a jar, which I guess is how they see us.

The other eye risked it and opened; the tiny creature came into focus.

She leaned forward, improving the view. "Where's the food?" she asked.

"Um, I don't know. I haven't been here long, I don't think." Somehow, I managed to sit up, while waves of magical energy made me urge even as I did my best to let it flow away as fast as possible, but the air was too full of it for me to control. Even the faery's presence was no longer enough to dispel the dreaded payback for use of dark magic.

There was too much in the room, and it was too concentrated—humans aren't designed to cope with such an onslaught of what isn't theirs by right of existence.

Merely being in the presence of a faery is enough to make you run screaming to an insane asylum unless you are powerful, and even then when they take you by surprise, and you haven't had time to prepare, it can be hit-or-miss if you can cope, let alone function.

But I'm Faz Pound, Dark Magic Enforcer, Peeker Down the Cleavage of Fae, Tickler of Tiny Ears, Licker of... you get the idea, and I've seen my share of fae. Just as well, because rescuing one a long time ago is what saved me from being forever enthralled by Ankine Luisi.

"I get food for faery," said the troll, seemingly having forgotten what happened.

"Ooh, goodie." The faery clapped her hands together in glee, sprinkling dust I stuck out my tongue to catch before she saw me and it blew away with a nod of her lovely head. Her wings beat faster, almost slicing my face to magic-encrusted ribbons.

"Hey, be careful." I retched one final time for luck, got to my feet awkwardly, and she took to the air. "You could have done that earlier," I moaned. My mouth felt drier than after sucking on an unripe apple then chasing it down with a generous helping of sand—that's what you get for eating troll.

"Done what?" She looked entirely relaxed, but was already losing interest in me.

I stared at her, trying to figure her out. With fae you can never tell if it's a trap or not. "You know, dealt with the succubus. I took a risk with the troll dust, wasn't sure if it would work, especially the second time."

She appeared confused for a moment, then shrugged—the usual fae attitude taking over. "Did something happen? Never mind, I smell food." She darted off, presumably to catch up with the troll.

"Stupid fae," I muttered, making sure she couldn't hear.

"I heard that," came her voice from somewhere at the back of the house, but also sounding like it was right in my ear. Magical after-effects made me too tired to care.

Fae are the worst for remembering things. No matter if you are human or entirely one of the true Hidden, you cannot expect to remember everything that happens if you lead a long, maybe infinite life. Fae, succubi, incubi, imps, goblins, trolls, and on the list goes, all are practically infinite beings, and it means they have to be selective.

Even long-living humans, or ex-humans, have to prioritize. I'm just over a hundred and have years, even a few decades, which are basically blank. For Mage Rikka, and ancient vampires like Taavi, they have the odd century that is gone forever. There is only so much you can keep, and the longer you live the more it gets sorted whether you like it or not. The important stuff remains, the day-to-day things, but events not deemed worthy get thrown on the scrapheap of memory.

I guessed what just happened was worth almost zero to the faery—I'd hate to see what was important.

A vision of Ankine Luisi remained in my mind. A scar on my memory that would never be wiped away. Her as her true self, with dark tattered wings, forked tail, the body all bone and stretched, mottled skin. No wonder she took on human form and reveled in the feel of female flesh of the soft and sensual kind.

Where exactly she was now I had no idea, but she wasn't next to me, and that was all I cared about right then.

The shamed Ambassador was still on the stairs. He was lost, unable to do much of anything now no longer enthralled. She had been all that had kept him going, now even that was gone. He was used up, a husk, no magic of his own left. It's impossible to know how he had allowed himself to get taken by her, but I guess she was just too powerful. She almost had me, so I can't exactly judge.

There was nothing I could do for him, so I sat down next to the empty man and gave my body permission to relax. Slowly, my mind unburdened itself as the dark magic slid back into the Empty. Little remained now, just me, a dark magic enforcer who was spent, a once powerful wizard with a bright future ahead of him who was lost, and dust on the carpet.

"You want eat?" The troll was in front of me, holding out a silver platter with an assortment of meats, bread, and fruit. The faery was stood on a slice of ham, tearing pieces off and ripping into it with teeth as sharp as needles, wings tucked away neatly.

"Why not?" I got up, and followed them into the dining room where I sank gratefully into a chair at an immaculately laid table, ready for guests that would never come.

I dragged out my phone and tapped a button. "You better come over to the Finnish Embassy," I said. "And bring some trolls. There are a lot of books that need moving."

"You okay?" asked Rikka.

"I've been better, but it's done."

"That's my boy. I never doubted you, Spark. Now, I just heard from the goblins, and they have a bit of a problem with—"

I hung up and ate an apple.

The End

Book 2 in the series is Evil Spark.

Get new releases first, and at a discount, via the Newsletter at www.alkline.co.uk.

Made in the USA
San Bernardino, CA
21 September 2016